PIRAT'S EARLY CASES

In which our hero yet again fails to appear

First published 2016

ISBN: 9781530449217

© Rob Falconer 2016

Rob Falconer has asserted his right under the Copyright, Designs and Patents Act 1988 to be the identified as the author of this work

All rights reserved

By the same Author:

**The Return of Inspector Pirat: His First Book
(published 2015)**

Paperback available on Amazon
www.amazon.co.uk/Return-Inspector-Pirat-First-Book/dp/1511429461/

eBook available on Amazon
www.amazon.co.uk/Return-Inspector-Pirat-First-Book-ebook/dp/B00UTKEKPM/

Visit Rob's website:
www.robertfalconer.co.uk/

For Valérie
for her constant support

Index

Preface

Chapter 1 – Hell's Waiting-room – a D.I. Pratt story

Chapter 2 - The Diary of Mary Beresford

Chapter 3 – The Wrong Case – a D.I. Pratt story

Chapter 4 – The Golden Fleece

Chapter 5 - Fred, a Stair, and Mrs. Rogers – a D.I. Pratt story

It's a Gift (a diversion)

Chapter 6 – The Face in the Foliage

Chapter 7 - Deep and Crisp and Evil – a D.I. Pratt story

Chapter 8 - RIP

Chapter 9 - The First of Criminals – a D.I. Pratt story

Chapter 10 – The Final Proof – a D.I. Pratt story

Beyond a Joke (a diversion)

Chapter 11 – Through a Glass, Lightly – a D.I. Pratt story

Chapter 12 – Dead and Breakfast

Chapter 13 – The Wrong Man – a D.I. Pratt story

Chapter 14 - You Hang Around Waiting for Hours … – a D.I. Pratt story

Chapter 15 – Requiem Symphony

In the Library with Theo Dagger (a diversion)

Chapter 16 - And Two Number 46 with Rice, Please – a D.I. Pratt story

Chapter 17 - The Toyshop that Moved

Chapter 18 - There's a Way – a D.I. Pratt story

Chapter 19 – Mrs. Gossip – a D.I. Pratt story

Chapter 20 – Off the Rails – a D.I. Pratt story

Preface

For those of you who have read 'The Return of Inspector Pirat: His First Book' (published in 2015, and available via Amazon), the format of this book should be immediately recognisable.

But those readers who only know Professor Guiteras as the eminent Professor of English Quixotisms at Pierrerouge College in Camford University may be surprised to know that he is also a well-respected author of detective fiction in his native Spain.

As it was felt that these stories of his should reach a wider audience, it was decided that a further selection should be made available to the English-speaking world.

This therefore is a second collection of Professor Guiteras' detective puzzles, a baker's dozen, thirteen, of which he wrote featuring his popular detective, Inspector Pirat.

As many of these involve essentially Spanish elements, I have taken the liberty, at the publisher's request, of changing these slightly, setting them mostly in Britain, against the quintessentially English background of the classic British detective stories that Professor Guiteras loves so much. I have therefore anglicised Inspector Pirat's name to Detective Inspector John Pratt.

I have also added a further seven of Professor Guiteras' short stories, mostly detective stories and puzzles, plus I have included three of his less serious short stories, which he called "diversions" (this term was particularly difficult to translate from the Spanish).

I might add that this publication is not being done at Professor Guiteras' request, as he seemed modestly not to wish these to be published outside Spain. However, the publishers and I believe that they do deserve a larger audience.

So, here is a collection of Professor Guiteras' earlier stories, as originally published in the Spanish-speaking world.

As with the first book, I have translated the contents from the original Spanish, even if I have no knowledge whatsoever of the language.

Rob Falconer
Penarth
2016

Editor's note: Despite all appearances, this preface forms part of the fiction.

Chapter 1

Hell's Waiting-room

Every year, Christmas was a grand occasion at Long Hall.

This year was to be no exception.

Lord and Lady Otterly's daughter, Celia, had invited four of her female friends along, and their son, Anthony, had invited four of his male friends.

Which greatly pleased Lord Otterly, as his memory was going. There was nothing he liked better than telling anecdotes over port after a grand meal, but he had recently been told off by Lady Otterly for telling the same stories over and over again. This Christmas, with eight people he had never encountered before, he would have no need to remember to whom he had told each particular story. Not that they wouldn't be bored anyway.

The visitors had been told to arrive punctually at two o'clock on Christmas Eve, and it was stressed how a lack of punctuality upset the hosts, so, bang on time (one suspected the cars had all been parked for some time just out of sight around the corner), four cars, of a quality rarely seen at Long Hall driving up to anything other than the tradesmen's entrance, appeared in a few puffs of black exhaust smoke on the driveway leading up to the stately pile.

The eight newcomers were met in the Grand Hall by Lord Otterly himself.

"Ahem. Welcome to Long Hall. Before our staff show you all up to your rooms, I rather thought I'd like to tell you a little bit about the building and its history."

Gloria, one of Celia's friends, commented sotto voce, "I didn't know you were open to the public, Celia. Does your father always conduct the tours personally himself?" She was rudely shushed by Celia.

Lord Otterly droned on. "The oldest part of the house was built in the Middle Ages, but was greatly expanded and modernised in the late seventeenth or early eighteenth century by a rich and eccentric industrialist, although some say he made most of his money from his involvement in the slave trade."

Credence to this was given by the fact that Lord Otterly had always refused to get involved with genealogists and had point-blank refused to be the subject of one of those family tree programmes that are so popular on television these days.

"Nevertheless, the house, although appearing fairly large on the outside, is in fact not that imposing. This is the Grand Hall, probably the only really impressive part of the building. To my right is the Ballroom, with a small theatre behind. To my left is the Green Banqueting Room ... I don't know why we call it the Green Banqueting Room, as it's the only one we've got ... and then, behind that, the Library, the Games Room, and some rooms that only the staff know about. But the thing first-time visitors always do, and I'm sure you have already done so, is to admire the sweeping staircase up to the first floor."

He waved his left arm expansively, but rather vaguely, towards the staircase behind him.

"The upper floor is symmetrically laid out. We have the two main bedrooms at the front, on either side of the hall, and then a series of five smaller bedrooms behind them. As we have another guest staying in the other large front bedroom, I'm afraid two of the men will have to share a room. I do hope that's all right with you."

As Lady Otterly had already pointed out, with Celia and four young female friends staying at Long Hall, along with Anthony and four young male friends, she was quite sure that no more than eight bedrooms would actually be needed ... perhaps even less, depending on the occupants' proclivities.

It was Gloria who piped up again, although this time her comments were directed to Lord Otterly. "Look, I know I'm not terribly good at calculations and that sort of thing, but isn't there a room over somewhere? If there are five smaller bedrooms on each side of the house, and there are eight of us, plus Celia and Anthony, then why do you say two of the boys have to share a room? Just do the math."

Lord Otterly smiled genially. "Actually, I was coming to that. Your mathematics seems exemplary, even if your English is clearly not up to much."

"Long Hall is reputed to be the haunt of quite a few ghosts and other supernatural phenomena."

Those who had previously wanted his Lordship to shut up and let them get up to their rooms now decided that they were quite happy enough to stay in the Grand Hall a little longer and listen to his Lordship.

"We have a Grey Lady, who is supposed to roam the West corridor upstairs. She is thought to be the ghost of a young Mary Westby, who died after eating a meal here. I have never seen her myself, but apparently she moans loudly, and constantly mutters threats to murder our cook."

"Then there is The Monk. Clad in dark habits and with a malevolent visage, this mediaeval monk can occasionally be glimpsed sitting in meditation in the Conservatory. Which is perhaps a little perplexing, as the Conservatory wasn't built until 1982, and was only added to allow a full-scale version of Cluedo to be played here."

It was Geraint who spoke up this time. "But what about the number of rooms?"

"Ah, yes," said his Lordship, "Hell's Waiting-room."

All ears were on his Lordship now. Even those who were ready for a toilet break stopped wriggling.

"This room is the one directly behind our room, which is above you to my right, on the west side of the house. It belongs to the original part of Long Hall that dates back to the Middle Ages. It has, or rather had, a rather pleasant view out towards the western side of the park."

"However, it is now permanently locked, and the only window is boarded up and securely nailed shut. The chimney has also been bricked up. "

"There had been rumours about the room for some time. Even in the earliest days of Long Hall, various people are supposed to have stayed in that room with mysterious consequences."

"But the modern legend only started at the beginning of the nineteenth century. A certain George Wilson stayed the night. He was a guest of one of the male heirs. He was not in his room when they went to see why he had not appeared for breakfast the next morning. Indeed, he was never seen or heard of ever again."

"Another guest, a Miss Violet Lamb, stayed there a few years afterwards. Again, no trace was ever found of her."

"The room was finally locked up after this, but one foolhardy guest tried to stay the night there without telling my forebears. When his plan was revealed, the staff were sent to get him out of the room. It was before midnight, but his hair had already turned white, and he had to be admitted to a lunatic asylum."

"There have been no such, er, problems since, as the room has been completely sealed off, and nobody has been allowed to stay there."

"And no ... unfortunately, I cannot vouch for any of these stories. They have been handed down from one generation to the next, and I have always wondered myself whether some of them were merely invented to keep the children out of the room."

Everyone who had gathered in the Grand Hall now took a long hard look at the room that was known as Hell's Waiting-room, none of them even considering that they might have been told the story for the same reason as his Lordship had just suggested.

There was one final comment from Lord Otterly. "Oh, I think I mentioned we have another guest staying in the front bedroom to my left. His name is John Pratt. Perhaps I should mention that John is a detective inspector in the Alefordshire Constabulary, should you find the need for conversational gambits."

The youngsters all looked blank.

Lord Otterly nodded. "And now, my staff are here waiting to take you to your rooms."

One ancient liveried footman appeared, and guided them arthritically up the stairs.

Anthony was sharing with Geraint, whilst George, Busby and Dick occupied the other three available rooms on the west side of the house.

Celia, Gloria, Fenella, Lavinia and Debbie each had their own rooms on the other side of the house.

And everything seemed to go well.

At first.

The meal that evening was designed to be not too sumptuous, so that the main meal on Christmas Day could easily eclipse it in terms of taste, luxury, and expense. But it was well-received even by the youngsters, although Debbie was heard to mutter quietly that she normally had a Chinese take-away on Christmas Eve, but it was OK as this was almost as good.

Then there were lots of the sort of games one is supposed to believe take place at grand country mansions when guests are present, and which the new guests were surprised to find actually took place.

There was snooker, charades, bridge, and a myriad board games, none of which were in the usual cardboard compendia that most of the youngsters were familiar with, and almost all of which were of the hand-carved variety.

Later, the menfolk retired for port in the Library on the ground floor. The guests were relieved to find that it contained large numbers of video cassettes, DVDs and CDs, plus a book.

Christmas Day at Long Hall dawned late for most of the inhabitants.

Around six a.m., the grandfather clock in the Grand Hall chimed, and that was the only sound to be heard. The staff were trained to be as quiet as possible.

The house did eventually liven up, but not until well after nine o'clock.

The buffet breakfast was a hit with the youngsters. "Just like an all-you-can-eat," said Debbie.

However, most of the kedgeree was left untouched.

And Christmas Dinner was the success Lord and Lady Otterly had hoped for, although the contribution by the cook and her kitchen staff was not referred to.

But then, at five, after more drinks and a refusal by the guests to return to the board games and charades of the previous night, things took a more sinister turn.

Anthony announced that Busby had decided to stay the night in Hell's Waiting-room.

His parents desperately tried to convince Anthony that he should dissuade him. But Anthony insisted Busby would not change his mind.

His Lordship confided to his wife that all would be well, as there was almost certainly nothing in the story whatsoever. She looked unconvinced.

There had been an old hunting-horn hanging in the Library. This Anthony had appropriated, and now it boomed forth throughout the house.

Anthony stopped to cough the dust out of his lungs.

Everyone downstairs stopped whatever they were doing, dashed into the Grand Hall, and looked up towards the boys' rooms.

Another strident blast boomed around the house, following by some even more strident coughing.

Suddenly, the boys appeared.

Dressed in their dinner jackets, Anthony and the others were carrying Busby's bed along the landing, it has to be said a little jerkily. Everyone had noticed that Geraint had been walking rather stiffly after pulling a muscle falling off the sofa the previous night when performing his charade of 'Titanic' whilst more than a little inebriated.

But all eyes were quickly drawn towards the pyjama-clad figure on the bed. He was laughing and waving at the others assembled on the ground floor, his flame-coloured hair flopping about untidily as it always seemed to.

Despite her fears for Busby, Lady Otterly's main concern initially was that they had given Busby the smallest and least-used room, and that the bed there was simply a wrought-iron contraption with a thin mattress. She hoped nobody would notice.

The entourage trooped into the forbidden bedroom, waited a few seconds, and then Anthony, Geraint, George and Dick emerged grinning, still carrying the bed, but without the mattress.

"You haven't left young Busby in there?" boomed her Ladyship. The iron bedstead was clearly too thin to hide him.

"He's OK. He's safe and sound in Hell's Waiting-room." replied Anthony. "Well, Dad said not to take the story too seriously. Don't worry. He'll be fine!"

And with that, Anthony turned the key in the lock, and the four of them just leant on the banister, apparently just waiting to see what would happen next.

"Give me that key at once," demanded her Ladyship, her viciously upper-class accent slipping for a few seconds.

Anthony complied, tossing it deftly downstairs into his father's hand.

"Anyway, now that there are only four of us," said Anthony, "I think we'll all go for a game of tennis. With Busby hanging around, there were just too many of us."

Suddenly, there were screams and a violent hammering coming from the direction of Hell's Waiting-room.

"Come on!" yelled Lord Otterly, as he and those standing around him thundered upstairs.

As his Lordship's group rushed upstairs, Anthony and his friends were coming downstairs. The noises had at least stopped.

His Lordship turned the key, and was about to enter the room when there was a strident yell.

"Hold on there!"

John Pratt had, up until now, been watching from the back of the group, but he now pushed forward towards his Lordship.

"I've been involved in too many cases to know you shouldn't go in without a witness and without wearing gloves. And I have two pairs of disposable gloves in my pocket!"

He produced them as might a magician.

The two entered the room cautiously.

As Lord Otterly had said, the room had been emptied of all furniture, so that all that was in the room now was poor Busby's mattress on the floor. It was very thin, and would certainly not be able to conceal a human body. The window was nailed shut, as Lord Otterly had said. And dust was thickly laid all over the floor, except for a number of footprints from the door to where the mattress had been placed. There were no other marks anywhere else.

And of Busby there was not a trace.

"We'd better not venture in any further," whispered John. "The officers in the official investigation will want to make a thorough inspection."

Neither Lord Otterly nor his wife really wanted the Police to be involved, but they realised they would have to be phoned. Anthony and his friends were of no help at all, as they were not to be found on the tennis court, and must have roamed farther afield.

Whilst the police officers were investigating the room, Lord Otterly and John were to be found deep in conversation in Lord Otterly's bedroom.

"I had a word with the Detective Inspector in charge," said John, "And he confirms the window is firmly nailed shut and has not been tampered with, the walls, floor and ceiling are all solid, and the fireplace has no working doors or hatches. And there are no priest holes either."

"Getting back to the original reason for the rumour, I agree it could either be genuinely supernatural, or a tale to keep others, perhaps children, out of the room, or a way of murdering people you want to dispose of."

"What!" said his Lordship, jumping slightly.

"Well, there are plenty of stories of landowners in the Middle Ages killing some rival for land or money, or because they opposed some plan of theirs, or to gain political power. What better way than to have a room with a secret hatchway in the fireplace, so that the intended victim could lock himself in, and then agents of the landowner could enter via the hearth, drag him off, and then kill or imprison him at their leisure."

Lord Otterly looked confused. "But I thought the Police chappie said the fireplace didn't conceal a hatch?"

"Not now, maybe, but perhaps at one time."

John wandered over to the fireplace. He ran his fingers along the stonework.

"There are definite grooves here, so perhaps there was an entrance into the next room at one time. It doesn't look as if it would work nowadays though."

"So what do you think, then?" Lord Otterly asked, frowning.

"Right, if Busby's disappearance wasn't supernatural, and he wasn't dragged through this hatch, then what's left?" asked John rhetorically.

"A young man is carried on a bed into a room without furniture and without any means of exit other than the door, the mattress is put on the floor, nobody wanders anywhere else in the room, and then the bed is taken out and the door is locked. And there is no way that the bed-frame or mattress could conceal a person."

Lord Otterly looked worried. "So it was supernatural then?"

John ignored him. He continued, "Were invitations posted to the visitors staying here?"

"Of course. I don't have a secretary any more, but my Butler, Blight, handles all that sort of thing. Do you want to meet him?"

"Yes, I think I rather should…" said John thoughtfully.

After two phone calls, one to Directory Enquiries, John returned to Lord Otterly's bedroom.

"All sorted," he said.

Lord Otterly nodded. "Good. Have you told the police officers?"

John nodded. "Yes, they've gone home now. They were rather upset."

Lord Otterly nodded. "Yes, I suppose it's not very easy to fill in official reports when someone's been done away with by a ghost."

"Done away with by a ghost?" John spluttered.

"I think it's time to explain," he said.

"Look, all that happened was that the lads got together and decided to frighten you by saying that Busby was determined to stay in Hell's Waiting-room … and then he'd vanish."

"But, of course he couldn't …"

"… Because he was already on his way home."

"What!" exclaimed Lord Otterly.

"Yes, Busby is back home with his family. He had a phone call this afternoon to say his mother was very ill, so he went straight home."

"That's awful!" exclaimed Lord Otterly.

"Oh, it's OK," said John in a calming voice. "She's much better now."

"No, I mean it's awful that we were fooled into believing he'd been done away with. Especially after we'd seen it all with our own eyes."

"Actually, it was quite a simple trick," explained John.

"Anthony, Dick and George carried the bed in, with Geraint sitting atop wearing a wig that Anthony would have had no problem finding in the props of the small theatre at the back of the house."

"And the fourth member of the group carrying the bed would have been another prop from the theatre, a dummy, possibly inflatable, dressed in Geraint's dinner jacket, but with its left arm tied to the bed and with its left leg linked to George's. As it was tied to the bed on the side away from the onlookers, they wouldn't have realised."

"Once inside the room, they merely dumped the mattress on the floor, they put Geraint back into his dinner jacket, and then they carried the bed-frame out and waited on the landing for your reaction. Geraint could easily have slipped into the room he shared with Anthony to get rid of the dummy and the pyjamas, and to hammer on the door and scream, making you all think the sounds were coming from Hell's Waiting-room."

"In all fairness, I doubt they thought the whole thing through fully, and mightn't have realised that the Police would have been called."

Lord Otterly sat back thoughtfully.

"Well, boys will be boys, eh?"

He thought a bit more.

"But I rather think I ought to take back my Christmas present to Anthony of two cases of a rather good whisky."

He grinned.

Then he chuckled.

"And I shall send them to the local police station instead."

He chuckled again.

Chapter 2

The Diary of Mary Beresford

Wednesday, June 20

At last, everything seems to be turning out well for me.

My final examination for my B.Sc. degree is over, and I'm certain I've passed (and I am most definitely not usually a confident person) ... although I'm not quite sure how I managed it, especially after learning a few weeks ago that my dearest Uncle Harold (whom I had never met) had passed away and left me a lot of money and a huge mansion in Cornwall!

And, for the first time, I have found true love. A fellow-student, Richard, and I have become very close in the last few weeks, and we're to be married in a registry office next week.

Why a registry office? Well, neither of us have any family alive (at least, not since darling Uncle Harold passed away), and it's so much quicker, with far less fuss. And it's considerably cheaper – my new-found finances have yet to be sorted out properly.

Anyway, I'm motoring down to Cornwall - alone - first thing in the morning to take a look at the jolly old house.

Thursday, June 21

Before I set off, I had had a good look at a map of the area around the mansion (which is called Pencarreg). The estate seemed much smaller than I had imagined, or rather hoped, it would be.

After I'd driven through the splendidly impressive gateway, I realised the approach road had been designed to twist around, like a snake with epilepsy, to give the impression of the estate being much larger than it was. I knew the house lay at one point behind a row of trees, but it was difficult to see it as I drove along, so I stopped the car, and walked though the trees to get a better look, my first view of Pencarreg.

I was disappointed to say the least.

Although Pencarreg was very old, the rear elevation, which faced away from the sea, looked as if it had been made out of concrete. It was featureless and very bland. I began to understand why the trees had been planted so densely there.

The road now twisted around to the west before running alongside the sea-wall, and then along the front of the house. From this viewpoint, the building looked magnificent, if a trifle unkempt. This was obviously from where the original owners had wanted one to have one's first impressions of the house.

I fell in love with it at once.

I had been told that a Mrs. Spargo was looking after the place for a nominal salary, but it looked as if it were only her rooms that had even been cursorily cleaned.

Which brought up the question whether I should spend (waste?) a lot of money in renovating the old pile, or whether I should sell it for its potential as a country hotel, or … well, were there any other options?

Still, it was all mine at the moment. I resolved to spend our honeymoon here, although, if I neglected to do a bit of cleaning, it might turn out to be more like a dirty weekend.

Friday, June 22

Cleaning.

Saturday, June 23

Cleaning.

Sunday, June 24

Cleaning.

Monday, June 25

Cleaning.

Tuesday, June 26

If the above diary entries seem rather depressing, I should perhaps have added that I did spend a little time relaxing, getting to know the house and the estate, and touring the immediate vicinity.

The house was not too large, being more of a glorified manor house. However, it would hopefully be large enough to serve as at least a small country hotel. The area in front had clearly once been a cultivated garden, but had now surrendered itself hopelessly to the weeds. There was very little else to the grounds, as most of it had been used to make the strangely-snaking approach road.

On the other side of the sea-wall was a large bay, the entrance to which was directly opposite the house, but some considerable distance away. The nearest habitations were some two miles around the bay to the west, in a small village which consisted of a church, a pub and a scattering of small cottages. There were other cottages and farms on the surrounding hills.

Still, now it was time to return to London for the wedding. And to tidy myself up a bit!

But no, there was one other thing … something which I decided not to mention in last Friday's entry, but now feel I should.

I'm not entirely sure if I did see what I think I may have done.

What Mrs. Spargo referred to as "The Grand Staircase" in the main entrance hall was hardly grand   But it did have a suit of armour at the top of the first flight (I am certain it was only there because it was too heavy for Mrs. Spargo to carry it off and sell it).

I remember examining this suit of armour for a minute or two. Then I became conscious that someone or something was watching me.

I turned around and found myself looking towards a vague figure. It, she, seemed worried and upset. She may even have been wringing her hands. She appeared to be a young girl, perhaps younger mentally than physically. She walked slowly away from me down the stairs before fading away near the bottom. She had seemed more upset than I was.

Mrs. Spargo said she had never seen any strange phenomena (not that she pronounced it like that).

But it was enough to make me call into the local pub on one of my rambles around the area, and to enquire if anyone knew anything about a ghost at Pencarreg.

I was directed to an old man in a corner.

He said his name was Mr. Penhaligon.

He was fairly non-committal until I bought him the pint he was so clearly angling for.

"No, I've never heard of any ghosts or similar at or near Pencarreg. We're a fairly hard-headed lot down here."

He winked, and I was just about to ask him to pay for his pint. But he continued.

"However, I've always been a little suspicious of the story surrounding a young scullery-maid by the name of Mary Mahoney. She worked at Pencarreg around the middle of the eighteenth century, but she suddenly left her employment in the middle of the night, taking all her belongings, such as they were, and was never seen around here ever again."

"Then why," I asked, "Should her ghost still be here?"

Old Mr. Penhaligon tapped the side of his nose conspiratorially.

"I've always wondered whether young Master Richard may have got her," he hesitated here, "With child, and may have done away with her. There were some lovely rose gardens there then."

He nodded, and winked in a rather unpleasant way.

"Nothing was ever proved … and nobody was ever accused. But your story of seeing a ghost perhaps adds some weight to my little theory, eh?" he added.

Well, maybe I saw nothing anyway!

Wednesday, June 27

I arrived back in London in the early hours of this morning.

But, even after quite a few showers, I still felt dusty and grimy.

And my Wedding was to take place in a few hours!

(*Editor's note: various entries in the Diary solely relating to the Wedding itself have been omitted here*)

In the afternoon, Dick and I drove down to Pencarreg.

He loved it too, especially the theatrical approach. Our room was at least now neat and tidy. He expressed a wish (which I endorsed) that we should live here forever.

But, sadly, even my now-inflated bank balance would be insufficient to allow us to reside here for too long.

Thursday, June 28

Dick and I decided to take a drive around the bay. He loved the pub! Mr. Penhaligon didn't seem to be in that day.

Friday, June 29

Thinking back, I hadn't realised that it was in fact exactly a week ago, at four in the afternoon, that I had had my first meeting with Mary Mahoney (for indeed it was she, I am now convinced).

I was sitting on a settee in the main hall, in front of some huge mullioned windows (Dick was fiddling with the car), when the room suddenly felt cold. The old grandfather clock which I had had some success in repairing chimed four o'clock.

Mary walked across from the kitchen and stood a couple of feet in front of me. She was looking at the floor at first, and then she raised her head. She looked so worried. She was definitely wringing her hands this time.

Was she condemned to roam this earth because of the injustice that had been done to her by the heir to Pencarreg? Was she so worried that her murder would never be acknowledged?

Should I try and find out the truth?

"I'll do it," I cried, and Mary vanished.

Saturday, June 30

What had once been a rose garden was now a matted mess of weeds. But the only part that would have been cultivated was actually quite small.

Dick had had to drive back to London (some honeymoon!) for a few days. His uncle (not as well-off as mine) had passed away, and he was the only relative able to meet the solicitor and sort out various legal problems.

So, whilst he was away, I resolved to dig up as much of the old rose garden as I could.

The weather was thankfully none too hot, but it was back-breaking work. I noticed Mary Mahoney wasn't around to help.

After a few hours, during which I unearthed nothing of any interest even to a trained archaeologist, I gave up.

I felt I had failed Mary!

Monday, August 02

Dick found he would be detained for longer than he had expected in London, so I decided to travel to the local county town, and check in the reference library for details of Mary's disappearance. If Pencarreg continued to be a drain on our resources, I might have to get used to travelling everywhere by bus!

Of course, as no crime had been alleged, there was nothing at all in the local press about Mary's disappearance. It was not as if she had stolen anything.

I did learn one thing though. Pencarreg was in such a remote area that travelling on the infrequent and meandering bus service would be something to be avoided as much as possible.

Friday, August 06

I see I've written nothing in my diary since Monday.

All I have done all week is to tidy things in the house a bit more, and try and see if I could find any clues in the front garden. There was nothing I could see there, but a good digging is something the ground could certainly do with.

To tell the truth, all I have been doing is waiting for Friday, to see if Mary would make another appearance at four in the afternoon.

And she didn't let me down!

Again I sat on the settee in the main hall, in front of those huge mullioned windows. At precisely four o'clock, I realised I could just make her out on the other side of where the old rose garden had been, sitting on part of the old seawall defences. But that was not even part of the garden. Why was she there?

I managed to find my old pair of binoculars, and focused on her.

She was sitting there unmoving. But she was not wringing her hands this time. She was just staring fixedly ahead, almost as if she were resigned to my not finding her body.

She had to have a decent burial!

I decided to go to her.

But I had to get my coat first. By the time I had reached the nearest part of the garden, she had vanished.

I rushed to the seawall, but she was nowhere to be seen.

I even looked over the wall to the rocks below, but there was nothing.

Perhaps I was getting obsessed with this apparition .

If it were real …

Still, Dick was coming back the following week.

Our belated honeymoon could start at last.

Friday, August 13

Again, I see I have written nothing in my diary since last Friday, the last time I saw Mary.

For once, my life has not been obsessed with ghost-hunting.

After dealing with his uncle's estate, Dick finally came back mid-week. All my time was spent in getting things ready for him, and then being with him. Just the two of us at last.

So, this time, Friday at four o'clock crept up on me without my realising.

I had in fact been spending a lot of time in the garden, but attending to the borders, rather than hunting for corpses in the old rose garden.

Despite forecasts of extremely bad weather (well, this was Cornwall!), we ventured into the garden, me because I wanted to show Dick my gardening handiwork, he because he had bought a new DSLR camera in London, and wanted to try it out on me, the house and, especially, the approaching storm.

I didn't even think we might be able to photograph a ghost!

We wandered along both borders either side of the old rose garden, and then finished up at the seawall. Looking over the top, we could see the lowering clouds as the storm began gathering force at the far end of the bay. The eye of the storm would be with us soon, but not, hopefully, before we had had time to rush back into the house.

I had brought my old cheap digital camera at Dick's request, I think so he could show me how superior the photographs were on his new DSLR.

It had been cold all day, but suddenly it got very cold indeed.

The dark, threatening clouds were now moving quickly around the bay. We could hear thunder. There were occasional flashes of lightning.

Even at that distance, we could hear a loud crack as a tree was hit near the village.

Now it was really cold.

"Look how black the clouds are now," Dick yelled above the noise. "Use your camera! Now!"

I looked across the bay. It was certainly dramatic, but I wasn't sure my camera could capture the drama and power of the weather.

I was looking through the viewfinder when my eye dropped to the date and time. It was Friday, August 13 at 1600 hours!

I suddenly thought of Mary, whom I had totally forgotten about.

Our "appointment"!

Was I so fickle that, now I had Dick back again, I could forget all about her?

Suddenly I felt a gust of wind, a chill blow, near my left shoulder, and turned, still looking through the viewfinder.

Mary was there!

She was now back as I had originally seen her, worried and agitated.

In fact, she seemed petrified!

She was fidgeting and looking around nervously.

She was constantly moving, darting from one side of my field of vision to the other.

Suddenly she pointed over my shoulder.

Her mouth opened. She looked terrified.

I dropped my camera on its strap, and turned around.

Dick was standing directly behind me.

He had put his new camera down carefully on the wall behind him.

He looked very intense and focused.

I remember the wind was blowing his long hair all over the place.

His eyes had a wild look.

And he had a large stone in his right hand.

He swung his arm down quickly, aiming for my head.

I moved suddenly.

He lost his balance and fell against the seawall.

I tried to grab his hand, but he plunged over the wall onto the rocks below.

I just had time to see his bloodied body before the waves swept him out to sea.

Did I move suddenly or was I pulled?

Postscript

I suppose I should have sold the house, bearing the mind the dreadful events that had occurred there.

But I had fallen in love with the place, and, by working very hard and opening the place to the public, and making jam and chutney, and occasionally letting a few rooms, and allowing film and television companies to film location work there … well, I doubt anyone with a fair amount of money in the bank has ever worked so hard. But it was the only way to keep the house.

And I loved every minute of it.

And Mary?

Mary!

Mary.

I never did dig up that rose garden. Tourists are told it's called the Wilderness. I usually make up some story about an heir to the estate having found his bride-to-be dying there and having decreed that it should remain uncultivated for all time.

So I never did find Mary's body there, nor anywhere else on the estate.

And I never did see her again.

Ever.

Chapter 3

The Wrong Case

When it was announced that there would be a new system of "hot desking" in the office in which D.I. John Pratt worked, everyone was much impressed that a concept as modern as that was being introduced. In fact, of course, all it meant was that everyone had to book sessions on the only computer (and the only desk) in the room, and the desks were sold off for firewood and replaced by uncomfortable but trendy Scandinavian chairs (no-one could work out why they were all marked with the name 'Bøgbut.')

So, John was perfectly happy to leave the office when summoned by his boss. His session on the computer wasn't due for another two hours anyway.

"This looks, or rather looked, more or less open-and-shut," said his boss.

"Harvey Williams was pretty rich, but didn't like to show it. He had lots in the bank, but usually wore the cheapest clothes, and his home, Wellesley House, although built in a fairly grand style a century or so ago, was in a bad state of decoration. The local constables described it as "squalid." He had only the minimum of furniture, and what he had was cheap. There were no luxury goods, electrical items, televisions, or anything like that in the house. His only interests in life appeared to be making money, not showing it, and sailing."

"Anyway, he died around a week ago, not unnaturally in a local sailing accident. It happens all the time I suppose, but, there again, anyone who wanted to dispose of him might think that as well."

"So it all looked above board and straight-forward, and we were ready to close the investigation, until ..."

He handed over a letter to D.I. Pratt.

"The fingerprint boys and handwriting experts have all had a look at it, and it's definitely written by Williams. There's absolutely no doubt about that. It's no hoax."

The letter was dated a month previously.

It read, "To whom it may concern. I am writing this and entrusting it to a friend with instructions to send it to the Police should anything suspicious happen to me within the next twelve months. I have reason to suspect that a certain individual may have designs upon my life, and have therefore decided to hide some incriminating evidence. I have hidden this in a metal box, which I have buried under the lawn to the south of Wellesley House. It is to be found under a flagstone on the north-east side of the clock."

John read it a few times. It had been typed in capital letters on a very ordinary piece of A4 that had been printed on a computer printer.

"It all seems very clear and precise," he said. "But, in that case, why haven't your men been able to find it?"

John's boss squinted slightly, as if someone had suddenly switched on a bright light. "They have looked, but they can't find a thing. However, the ground quite clearly had not been disturbed for at least a month or so, so it looks unlikely that anybody has already found the box and removed it. I thought perhaps you might want to go down to Wellesley House this afternoon. It isn't far away."

As the site would by now have been subjected to the excavations of a considerable number of policemen and other official investigators, John didn't think there was much chance of his finding anything, but, against his better judgement, found himself nodding.

He copied down the main details of Harvey Williams' letter into his notebook, and, having been handed a map, set off for Wellesley House immediately. It wasn't until he left the building that he realised he hadn't asked why anyone would have a clock on their lawn.

Wellesley House was a large and crumbling red-brick mansion of indeterminate vintage. Once, no doubt, quite impressive, it was now sadly deteriorating, and a number of small trees could be seen growing out of the upper walls.

There was only one lawn, to the south, as set out in the letter. The lawn ran from the house for some distance towards a river, called the Swaithe according to the map, which formed the southern boundary of the property.

Right in the middle of the lawn, facing the house, was a large floral clock, surrounded by flagstones. It now served solely as a reminder of past glories, as it was badly overgrown and neglected. However, it was still a prominent feature of the lawn, its position having been made even more prominent by its being cordoned off by metal stakes and plastic tape warning the public not to enter. The expected throng of eager members of the public was not in evidence, however, and there was no-one in sight.

A few worm-hunting blackbirds flew away as John approached.

Inside the cordon, John could see that, not only had the flagstones to the north-east been lifted, but, in fact, all of them had been removed by his colleagues. However, his boss had said that they had taken care to examine the area beforehand, and had confirmed that no-one appeared to have disturbed the ground for a month or so, which would be roughly since the box was buried, according to the letter Harvey Williams had written.

And that's all there was to it, John thought. The letter had been quite clear, and yet there was nothing under any of the flagstones. Without even bothering to get his hands covered with soil, he sat down on a convenient bench, took out his mobile phone and phoned his boss.

"Look, there's no point in my wasting my time down here. The letter's perfectly clear, and our boys have been pretty thorough. There is no way that they could have missed the box if it was put where Harvey Williams said he put it ..." He paused for a moment and surveyed the lawn in the immediate vicinity of the clock, where the turf had been torn up and what looked like extensive archaeological excavations had taken place over a considerable area. "... Or within a ten-metre radius for that matter."

"Hold on, though ..." He thought for a while, even though he could feel his boss's impatience almost tangibly at the other end of the line.

"You said Harvey Williams lived in squalor and had no electrical equipment or anything like that. Yet he had a computer ... and, yes, why did you get the handwriting experts to look at the letter if it was printed from a computer?"

He didn't wait for his boss's reply, "The original was hand-written in mixed case wasn't it? It was only a copy that you showed me?"

His boss sounded bored, "Well, there didn't seem any need to let you see the original ..."

John switched off his phone, in disgust with his boss and with himself for not thinking of it earlier. He looked around the gardens.

The lawn was largely featureless except for the clock. There were arboreta to the west and east, and on either side of the lawn were lily-covered canals leading towards the end of the lawn, which overlooked the River Swaithe.

John looked at the details of the letter he had written in his notebook for a minute, yelled "And Harvey Williams liked sailing!" and then raced off towards the river.

The River Swaithe was wide here, and its current fairly slow and leisurely. It seemed perfect for a relaxing afternoon fishing or just pottering about in a boat.

There were no boats moored here now, but there was a small private quay leading off the river into the grounds of Wellesley House.

"And there are flagstones around the quay," John muttered aloud.

"If whoever transcribed Williams' letter mistook 'dock' for 'clock' ... I mean, a lower-case 'd' *can* look like 'cl' ..." he mused.

This time, he didn't worry about getting his hands dirty.

He lifted a flagstone on the north-east side of the dock, and poked a small stick into the soil, but found nothing.

He tried the next flagstone.

This time, he was luckier.

Underneath, below a few layers of earth was a metal box. It wasn't locked.

Harvey Williams had been an amateur blackmailer in a small way, with apparently only one client, albeit a rich one.

Full details were enclosed.

Fascinated, John read for a few minutes before phoning his boss.

Chapter 4

The Golden Fleece

"Well, it's an interesting story, but how the hell do you expect me to be able to tell you where the damned treasure is?" spluttered Dwight Barnes rather helplessly.

It was in the late 1940s. He was sitting in the corner of a bar in New York with one of his friends, Sam Smith. There were usually three others in the group, but only Dwight and Sam were there that morning.

Dwight had only one leg, after a car accident in his teens, and he had been unable to sign up with his four friends when America had joined the Second World War. All four had survived the war, but one of them, John Dain, had recently suffered a heart attack, and had died on a return visit to France.

"Hang on," muttered Dwight, "Here's The Professor. He likes conundrums, er, conundra. Why not ask him?"

Sam looked a little unsure about this, but reasoned that they had nothing to lose now.

Harry Klein, certainly not a real professor in any sense, was beckoned, and ambled over to the table where Dwight and Sam were sitting.

"You'd better explain it all from the start," suggested Dwight.

"Right. It's a long story and a bit sordid, I suppose."

"Myself and three others had been fighting in France for some time, but the end of the war was in sight, so we decided to try and make a little something out of it if we could. I mean, everyone was doing it, especially the Germans."

"We had the chance and we took it. We encountered a small German unit trying to make a getaway to one of the Atlantic ports. Look, to be fair to us, we had no idea what they were carrying, or whether they were guarding anything valuable at all, so I suppose it might have been some last-minute act of patriotism on our part."

"We saw them coming and decided to ambush them, and let's just say we won, killed all the guards, and luckily suffered no casualties ourselves."

"And we found ourselves the proud possessors of a quantity of gold bullion ... lots of it."

"We didn't know what we should do with it, and I don't suppose I really know now what we should have done, but what we did decide to do was to bury it and collect it later."

"We felt we could hardly smuggle it back when we returned with the Army, so we drove to a secluded but memorable spot to hide it until later."

"Although we'd been friends for years, suddenly none of us seemed to trust the others. As subsequent events proved, we were justified in our fears."

"We wanted to be able to bury our gold somewhere we could recognise perhaps even a year or two later, so we chose somewhere really distinctive. We drove to a crossroads we knew just a few miles east of the village of ... well, I don't think we need to know the name of the place, do we? There were no buildings there, just two roads intersecting almost exactly at right angles. They might have been Roman roads, they were so straight. The crossroads itself was on a slight hill, so each of the roads sloped gently away from it. There was a solitary telegraph pole at the crossroads, and below that was one of those shrines you find at quite a few dangerous junctions in France, although the way the French drive I reckon all junctions in France are dangerous. Anyway, this shrine was really unusual and distinctive."

"We decided to each take one of the roads, walk a reasonable distance along it, and then each bury our quarter of the gold fairly close to the side of the road. That way, we reasoned no-one would be likely to dig it up in the near future. I mean, it would be well away from agricultural land, and we didn't think anyone would be widening the roads in that remote place. Anyway, we reckoned France wouldn't have any spare cash for that sort of thing for some time."

"So we all started walking away from that shrine at the same time, one east, one north, one west, and me south. We knew we couldn't be seen from the other roads, because there were thick lines of trees alongside each road. It wasn't like the usual French avenues, with trees planted at intervals. These trees were planted thickly enough for each of us not to be visible to the others. So we felt safe that each of us knew only the location of our own treasure."

"After exactly thirty minutes - we had all agreed on the same time, so each of us wouldn't know how far the others had walked - we met up again at the crossroads, and resumed our duties as normal. In time, we returned to New York, and we decided to go back to France together after a suitable lapse of time. We knew that none of us could return without the others' knowing, because we usually meet here every evening, and, if one doesn't turn up, we find out why!"

"Anyway, we decided to return on the last Friday of last month. And we found out we'd been right not to trust even our best friends."

"John, John Dain, that is, left on the flight before the one we'd agreed on. I had booked the tickets for all of us, but John went behind our backs and bought a separate ticket for himself."

"We only found out when he didn't turn up at the airport. We couldn't do anything about it then of course, except not to waste any time, and to get straight to that crossroads. We had intended living it up in Paris for a few nights first, but, obviously, we ditched that idea."

"When we got to the airport in Paris, there was a message waiting for us. John had got there quite a few hours before us, but had had a heart attack in the lounge there. Serve him right, too. It must have been the thought of what he was doing to his friends that brought it on. He must have been conscious for a while, because he had left a message for us, to tell us where to find him, but he was already dead by the time we got to the hospital."

"I have to say that, even though we'd been friends for many years, we hardly grieved over him, after what he had tried to do to us."

"We didn't even stay the night in Paris, but pushed straight on for … well, that village, and, yes, we each found our own gold easily enough."

"Look, I'm not trying to be greedy, but we felt we should recover John's treasure too. He didn't have any close relatives, and so we felt we were entitled to it, especially after the way he'd treated us."

"So, we dug and dug all along both sides of his road from a short distance from the actual crossroads to as far as we felt he could have walked in that time, allowing time for the actual digging of course. And we found nothing. He could not have hidden it up a tree, there were no other buildings, and he certainly didn't bring it back with him."

"Have you any ideas?" Sam Smith said doubtfully.

The Professor pursed his lips.

"On the basis of that information, do you really expect me to?" he asked, a twinkle in his eye.

"Er, no," replied Sam, no twinkle in his eye.

"Well, actually, perhaps I have," smiled The Professor.

"The fact that he decided to jump the gun and catch an earlier plane indicates that he must have known more or less exactly where at least one of you had buried your gold. You see, he hadn't allowed himself much time to hunt around, had he?"

"And how would he have known that, eh? You said that no-one could have seen you from the other roads."

Sam shook his head vehemently.

The Professor allowed a considerable pause before continuing.

"Well, the only way would be if he had stayed back at the crossroads, and climbed up that telegraph pole, so that he could see exactly where each of you buried the gold."

"You said that the roads were straight, and that the telegraph pole was on the top of a small hill. If you couldn't have been observed from the other roads, you certainly could have been from the top of the pole. And I doubt whether you looked back up the road you were walking along, as you assumed all the others would be on their respective roads. Anyway, I think you would all have been too absorbed in your digging to have noticed a small distant figure up a telegraph pole, and that for only a few minutes, or even seconds."

Sam nodded in agreement.

"So that means he knew where each of us had buried the gold, but we have no way of knowing where his was buried."

He shook his head sadly.

"Not exactly," added The Professor.

"If he spent almost all of his allotted time near the pole, waiting to climb up it to check where you were burying your gold, he can't have moved far down his road, can he?

"You said you've looked along almost the whole length of his road, but have you checked right alongside the pole itself?"

"No!" yelled Sam

"I'm off to buy some airline tickets," he added, rushing out of the bar.

"I just hope he tells the others," said Dwight quietly.

Chapter 5

Fred, a Stair, and Mrs. Rogers

"I've just murdered an old lady," said Larry Sadd into his pint.

Even for a hotel-owner with falling receipts, V.A.T. and accounts to juggle, he seemed unnaturally gloomy. As his voice sounded serious, his friends felt they should reply as helpfully and sympathetically as possible, but could only manage "Are you certain?" and "Surely not?"

Larry appeared to ignore these responses, and continued, as if changing the subject, "No, it's the hotel. I always try to adhere to the Health and Safety rules and whatnot, but I think I must have fallen short of the requirements this time." He stirred his beer idly with a fountain pen. He didn't even notice when the top fell off into his beer.

"We were booked for a sort of family reunion last Saturday. It wasn't a particularly large family, but enough to reserve the function room and six suites" (Larry's hotel no longer appeared to have bedrooms, even if it had hardly changed over the years).

"You may remember Barry, one of my barmen." Larry must have been particularly preoccupied, as he normally referred to him as his sommelier. "Well, he was behind the bar adjoining the function room, where most of the family had congregated. They were awaiting the last few members before the festivities began in earnest."

"Anyway, he heard this almighty crash and a scream, as if someone had fallen downstairs. He opened the door that leads into the long corridor that runs towards the rear of the hotel. A short way along this corridor, some stairs lead off to the right, to the first floor bedrooms."

"Lying at the foot of these stairs lay Fred, one of the younger members of the family holding the reunion. He's about seventeen, I suppose. He was massaging his left elbow, and wincing."

"Barry said that Fred looked up and smiled, albeit a little grimly. He said that he was a little shaken, that's all, and that we needn't worry as he wasn't going to sue us. That was a relief anyway, but I wish Barry had got it in writing. All this rather surprised Barry, as his brief time with the youth had suggested his reaction would have been rather more aggressive. Fred said that there was no need for a medical examination, and that he'd just sit on a chair in the little alcove alongside the stairs for a few minutes to rest. But he waved Barry back to the bar, and told him to get the Manager - me, that is - because there was something wrong with the carpet at the top of the stairs, and he didn't want anyone else to fall. Barry tried to go and look at the carpet, but Fred was most insistent, and said *I* should be brought along to see to it *straight away*."

"I hadn't heard any of this. The bar where Barry was working lay between these stairs and the main part of the function room, but I was in the stock room, even farther away. The family hadn't heard anything either, as they were making a lot of noise.

"Anyway, Barry burst in and told me what had happened. I followed him immediately to the stairway."

"Just as I opened the door to the corridor, there was another crash. Barry said it seemed even louder than the first. This time, it was old Mrs. Rogers who came tumbling down the stairs, and she arrived at the bottom full pelt at about the same time as we did. She looked stone dead, but that's not surprising, considering the number of stairs there are."

"Fred limped out from the alcove beside the stairs, and let out a yell when he realised it was one of his family who had fallen downstairs, and, of course, all the rest of the family then rushed out from the function room."

"As Mrs. Rogers was obviously dead, I wasn't sure whether to call a doctor or the Police, but in the end we called both, and then I left Barry with the, er, corpse. Some of the female staff were given the job of trying to soothe everybody. I went to have a look at the carpet at the top of the stairs (as the Police did later). Some of it was certainly loose. It may be wishful thinking, but it looked to me as if someone had tampered with it."

"I was naturally worried about how all this was going to affect me. Luckily, I saw Doctor Shakespeare arrive with the police officers, and I know him fairly well (actually he's in the same Rotary Club as I've been trying to get into)."

"I phoned him up later on, and asked him what would be in the report he'd be submitting. Apparently, the old dear had terrible injuries. She must have been pretty frail, as her injuries had been extensive even allowing for the large number of stairs involved. But he said he was almost 100% certain that the injuries hadn't been caused by anything other than falling downstairs. He also said it didn't seem as if she had fallen that fast, as she appeared to have rested momentarily on the third step from the bottom - there was a small pool of her blood there - before she collapsed down the last few stairs. Fred's injuries were much less, basically a very badly sprained ankle, but there again he is much younger."

"None of this cheered me up, as you can expect. I'm now awaiting a visit from the Health and Safety people, or the Police, or whoever deals with these things. No-one's cancelled any bookings yet, thank God."

Up to this point everyone had remained respectfully quiet. Now Larry's three companions realised that Larry clearly felt that it was their turn to make a contribution to the conversation.

Herbie Dann was a local greengrocer and used car dealer. He was also a keen reader of detective fiction. He cleared his throat noisily, and looked around the table. All eyes were on him. "I'm off for a pee," he intoned. "Ask Pratt." He shuffled off towards the back of the pub.

Grantley Armitage was a crime reporter on the local newspaper, 'The Alefordshire Gazette' (he usually dropped the 'ette' to make the paper seem more trendy). It was now his turn to clear this throat and look knowingly around the table. "I'll join you, Herb," he called, and careered off towards the toilets. "Ask Pratt," he yelled over his shoulder.

Only John Pratt still remained.

Detective Inspector John Pratt was a member of the Aleford CID.

He cleared his throat a little louder than the others had done.

"So, you want to find out if there's an alternative version of events that reflects a little less culpably on your hotel, eh?" It was clearly meant as a rhetorical question.

Larry nodded glumly, clearly not expecting much.

"Who would have been in that part of the hotel at the time?" John asked.

"Well, the family had already made quite a few head counts to check who was missing. They were only waiting for Fred and, er, the late Mrs. Rogers."

"It seems to me that there are a few possibilities, each of which more or less fits the details you've given," he said slowly. "What we have to do is decide which is the most likely."

"What makes me suspicious of young Fred's story, apart from his apparent change of personality, is that his injuries seemed to have changed within a short period of time. It was originally one of his elbows that was hurting, whereas it was actually his ankle he had badly sprained."

"Also, Mrs. Rogers arriving at the foot of the stairs at exactly the same moment as you turned up seems well-engineered."

"But, mainly, that small pool of blood on the stairs worries me."

"I suppose the whole thing could be exactly as is supposed to have happened. The carpet could have became damaged in one of many ways, although each might ultimately be your responsibility." He looked up to check that Larry's twitch had started, and was well-rewarded. "Young Fred might have fallen downstairs, but come to little harm, being young and fit and perhaps even a little inebriated even at that time of the day."

"But that doesn't really explain the blood on the third stair. If Mrs. Rogers had come down the stairs at such a speed as you said she did - and that would seem to be consistent with her injuries - surely she couldn't have rested near the bottom long enough to leave any trace of blood, let alone a small pool?"

"It also doesn't explain the extent of Mrs. Rogers' injuries."

"No, no, I think that the most plausible theory is that Fred pushed Mrs. Rogers down the stairs *both times*."

Larry Sadd opened and closed his mouth a few times, but said nothing.

"I don't know what dear Fred's motive might have been. Perhaps an expected bequest, revenge, or whatever. I don't know."

"He would have loosened the carpet first, of course, and then pushed the old dear down the stairs."

"Even her frail body would have made a considerable din as she cascaded down the stairway. But, horror of horrors, despite her fearful fall, he sees that she's not dead. She's still moving slightly at the foot of the stairs."

"Unsure what to do, he comes down to examine her. How can he finish her off without adding suspiciously to her injuries? He certainly wouldn't want her to live now, as she would be able tell everyone exactly what had happened."

"Having decided on a course of action, he starts to carry her upstairs, but has to put her down on the third stair when he hears Barry arriving. He tells Barry it was he who fell downstairs. As he obviously doesn't want Barry to see the old lady on the stairs, he insists on his returning to fetch you immediately."

"He then takes the body up to the top of the stairs again."

"For extra authenticity, he decides to wait for a witness ... you. I don't know whether there's a mirror at the foot of the stairs that would show when the door to the function room opened, but the increase in volume when that happened would probably have been sufficient warning of your imminent arrival. As soon as he knows you're approaching, he gives Mrs. Rogers the fatal push, probably harder than the first time."

"This time it works. He then drops down the side of the staircase into the alcove below. This is presumably a considerable distance, which would explain his ankle injury."

"I think you'll find that that theory fits the facts better than any other explanation, and anyway I think it's the *only* way to fully explain some of the evidence."

Larry had begun to brighten up as he listened to John.

Now he nodded happily. "Yes, if I discuss this with the Doctor, I'm sure he'll agree that it fits in better with his findings."

Larry nodded again and beamed. "If you ever want to stay at my hotel, John, you can stay for fr ... er ... a 5% discount," he added magnanimously.

John settled back into his seat, as the other two returned from their rather protracted visit to the toilets.

What he had neglected to tell Larry was that he thought he might find it very difficult to convince the Police that they should think the case any more complex than the simple case they originally thought it was.

Nobody likes extra work.

It's a Gift

A diversion

It all started on the Monday I had my first premonition.

I sat down at the breakfast table and said to my wife, "Ethel, I have a feeling my life is going to change for the better as from today."

"I am going to win something," I added.

It wouldn't be anything new for me to be entering competitions. I do that all the time. What would be novel would be for me to actually win something worthwhile. I had been comping, as I believe the term is, for more than five years, despite never having won anything at all ... or rather, nothing except for a tyre pressure gauge. Not that I'd actually wanted to win that. I had been aiming for the first prize, a gleaming new Ford Focus. "Now you'll have to win a car to go with it," suggested Ethel, which, for her, was quite witty.

There was a tap at the door. That was unusual in itself, as the postman usually just pushes the post through the letter-box. We never receive anything bulkier than a plastic bag to fill for some charity or other.

Harry, our postman, stood on the door-step, holding a parcel. "Looks interesting," he said, fondling and feeling the parcel as if it were a Christmas present for him.

"Thanks," I said, shutting the door more than a little rudely.

I sat down at the table and unwrapped the parcel eagerly.

There was a letter congratulating me on winning a prize in the City Nappy competition (and no, we don't have any children). Third prize wasn't wonderful. It was just a small battery-operated alarm clock with a digital display. But, to us, it represented the acme of competition prizes. In fact, I had every reason to be happy with the alarm clock, considering the poor tie-breaker I'd submitted, a poem based on a rather puerile pun on the company name.

And so, as I said, it all started that day. My life changed from that day forward.

Not in terms of winning competitions, I hasten to add. There was little chance of that ever happening, I'm afraid. No, my life changed in a completely different way.

I work for a well-known international firm of accountants, whose offices are luckily one bus-stop from where I live.

We usually stop for a tea break after we've been there for two hours or so, around 11.00 a.m.

"Sorry to hear about Danny Goole, eh," I volunteered.

"What about him?" muttered Harry Hollis, a colleague.

"He died last night," I replied.

Someone was prevailed upon to bring their newspaper over from another cubicle, and we read that he had been found dead of a suspected heart attack at 3.00 a.m. that morning.

The conversation turned in a general sense to Danny's sporting achievements, but I gradually drifted away from the talk.

How had I known Danny Goole was dead?

Since his demise at 3.00 a.m., I had not seen a newspaper. Neither myself nor Ethel take any newspaper these days, as the news always seems so depressing, and it was better, we felt, not to know too much about what was going on. I certainly had not read someone else's paper on the bus, indeed none had been in evidence. I hadn't seen a newspaper until one was brought over during the discussion about Danny Goole. And my hearing is so bad, I would have had no chance of eavesdropping.

I never watch television until I get home in the early evening, and we never listen to the kitchen radio before I leave for work. And no radios or internet usage are allowed in the office I work in.

So how had I known about Danny Goole?

My prediction about winning a prize in a competition became the first in a string of such premonitions.

The same thing seemed to happen almost every day from that point on. On each successive day that week, as soon as I got to the office, I was able to tell my colleagues about an earthquake in Chile, an explosion in the Middle East, the bankruptcy of a major company I used to work for, and a serious accident on the M1.

The following week I tried to be more careful.

I checked that the radio was off in the kitchen (I thought it might have been on quietly, perhaps just above my hearing threshold). I didn't take the bus in case I saw someone's newspaper. I made my walk a little longer in order to avoid any newsagent who might have the latest headlines written on a board outside. I checked there were no sources of news at the office.

In all fairness, these weren't entirely my ideas. My colleagues were clearly intrigued at my being able to predict the future (well, if not the future, certainly the very recent past). They made copious suggestions as to how I could better approach laboratory conditions, hence the changes to my daily routine.

And yet I still found I could tell my colleagues what had happened before anyone told me.

They became more and more insistent that I should tell someone in authority, perhaps in the medical profession, and test my abilities in a controlled scientific environment.

And so that's why I knocked on the door of Professor Eccles on the way home from work one evening.

Jeremy Street had been one of the colleagues at work who had been most vociferous that I should put my abilities to the test. His daughter was studying psychology at the local university, and he felt sure that one of her tutors, Professor Henry Eccles, would be interested in testing my abilities.

Jeremy knew his address, and so I called in to see if he were indeed interested in studying my case.

Professor Eccles' initial expression suggested disbelief or disinterest, but, after I had explained my apparent abilities in more detail, he finally invited me into his house.

Talking to Jeremy afterwards, I think that Professor Eccles' interest was largely because all the other professors in his department had just published books, and he hadn't. That he felt I might have been the source of any small degree of fame for him shows how desperate he must have become.

"If what you say is true," Professor Eccles intoned, "Then we need to apply laboratory test conditions before we go public on this."

He thought for a few moments.

"But I don't think we're ready to take you into the university yet. There would be unwarranted intrusions from my fellow psychologists, poking their noses into what is essentially my personal research."

He clearly came to a decision and nodded.

"Yes, you shall stay at my house for a few days, so that I can monitor your behaviour and control the stimuli you are presented with," he said. "Is tonight OK?"

I wasn't sure whether I had actually agreed to this or not, but my assent seemed to be tacitly assumed, and so I returned to Professor Eccles' house at 9.15 p.m. that evening with my pyjamas, toothbrush and so on. I was due some leave at work anyway.

My bedroom at Professor Eccles' house was quite austere. I felt it hadn't always been like that, as there were dust-marks on the sideboard where household items must have been at one time, and there were faded areas on the wallpaper. But clearly Professor Eccles wanted to remove as many stimuli as possible, so as to create a situation as close as he could to laboratory conditions.

If the room were bare and uninteresting, breakfast was not. It was very good, almost opulent, as appeared to suit the Professor's taste. There was music from his CD-player, but there were no radios or televisions in the house that worked. I later discovered that all the fuses had been removed from the plugs of anything that might transmit news.

After my first night, I was pleased to be able to report to the Professor that there might have been some sort of security scare at Heathrow. This turned out to be true, and, thankfully, it was only a scare (the usual unattended bag). He seemed impressed.

Things continued like that for the next few days. He seemed genuinely pleased with my performance, and at least I felt I was no fraud.

But could I only report on what had happened in the last few hours, or could I actually predict the future, or even near-future?

That is what he wanted to concentrate on in the next few sessions. He said he wanted to try and pinpoint the exact time I received, or became aware of, this information.

Or rather, it was what he was *hoping* to investigate, for, two minutes into our early-morning session on my first Wednesday there, there was a knock at the door, and the Professor's superior at the University appeared. He had two soberly-suited gentlemen with him. They looked as if they were from some Government department. The Professor clearly didn't want to let any of them in, including his superior.

"Look, I'm terribly sorry, Professor, but word seems to have got around about what you are doing in here, and now these two gentlemen and their department are interested." Professor Eccles' superior craned his neck around the edge of the door to try and see into the house. As he couldn't see anything of any interest, he merely shrugged and then walked a short distance away into the garden, leaving the two other gentlemen to start a deep conversation with Professor Eccles.

The Professor returned to me a few minutes later. "Sorry, but it seems that this is all out of my hands now. I can't hide you any more. These gentlemen would like you to go with them."

A voice called from the front door, "Tomorrow at nine will be OK. We're not living in some Communist regime." He sniggered as if this were a fine joke.

"Well, it seems I've only got you for a few more hours," Professor Eccles said resignedly. "Shall we try and wrap everything up by early tomorrow morning?" He smiled, probably for the first time since we'd met.

He worked harder with me that day than on any other day, and forgot all about lunch until I reminded him well past the middle of the afternoon.

Because he wanted to check my brain patterns, he had me wired up to some machine in the bedroom and checked the readings all the rest of the day and even most of the night. He said he wanted to see if there was any particular time when my brain patterns changed.

He woke me up much earlier than my usual eight o'clock. He had apparently only dozed fitfully during the night.

"OK, " he asked, "Anything? Did you feel or sense anything during the night?"

For the first time in weeks, I had had no dreams or premonitions whatsoever. I told him so. He seemed disappointed. He said he had hoped to make a breakthrough before he handed me over to the Government men.

I asked if he could disconnect me from his machine so I could go to the bathroom.

I left Professor Eccles sitting on the bed. It was now exactly eight o'clock.

The alarm clock which I had won and which I had brought from my house started up.

I could hear it from the bathroom.

"Good morning, and here is the eight o'clock news. There has been an air crash in the state of Wisconsin in America. At this stage, the fate of the passengers is not known …"

Chapter 6

The Face in the Foliage

"I understand you trace missing persons, Mr. Diamond."

It was in fact Sam Diamond's first week as a private investigator in his new office in Godalming, so Sam would have been willing to do just about anything in order to make a bit of money. Godalming seemed to be almost totally devoid of any interesting crimes, or indeed of any crime whatsoever, and Sam's once-large bingo win was rapidly diminishing.

And no, Sam Diamond was not his real name, but Simon Pretty didn't seem particularly appropriate for a private investigator.

Mrs. Dudley-Stewart repeated her statement, and Sam nodded, trying not to look too overenthusiastic.

Mrs. Dudley-Stewart's sell-assurance diminished slightly, "Er, even if they're only missing from a painting?"

Sam felt nonplussed, but managed to retain his composure. He really needed that money.

He nodded again.

"Call at this address," Sam's new client said, handing over a calling card. "I hope you're not going to be too expensive."

Sam parked his car around the corner from Mrs. Dudley-Stewart's house, not for reasons of discretion, but simply because he was ashamed of it.

The client's house suggested she need have no worries about paying anybody's fees. It was set well back from the road, and was built in a vaguely cottagey style, although it was far bigger than any cottage Sam had ever seen.

Although clearly old, the house had been updated with some very unsympathetic improvements, such as some unpleasant-looking modern double-glazing, and a new roof that just didn't fit in with the rest of the house.

Mrs. Dudley-Stewart opened the door herself, casually muttering something about it being "Maid's day off," although she wouldn't have fooled anybody.

Sam was shown into the front lounge.

"Is this where the, er, painting is … or was?" he asked, looking around.

Mrs. Dudley-Stewart pointed at a large picture on the rear wall. "That's the picture. I bought it just over a year ago. It seems to have been quite an investment. Anthony Bellini was a local man, at that time not well-known outside Godalming, so it didn't cost much, but luckily he died a year ago, and the value of his work has now literally shot up. It's worth thousands today. I only wish I'd bought more."

"Do have a close look at it," she implored.

The painting itself seemed positioned to catch the late evening sun rather than direct sunlight. It looked quite unremarkable, almost a copy of one of Monet's paintings of his garden at Giverny. It showed a small lake or pond, with an uninteresting bridge over it. There was a lot of similarly uninteresting foliage around. To Sam, having been brought up in the country with parents who were both keen gardeners, the flowers looked garish and the colouring seemed overemphasised.

"I can't see anybody in it," he said after a few minutes' scrutiny.

"Well of course you can't," said Mrs. Dudley-Stewart, as if speaking to a child. "I told you he'd vanished, didn't I?"

"What do you need to know?" she continued.

"Just the facts, ma'am," said Sam, who was a prominent member of the local Amateur Dramatic Society, and who was invariably cast as a detective even if the play didn't even remotely relate to crime.

"I bought the painting because I felt the poor artist was desperately in need of money. I never realised it would be worth this much. But it was only after a few weeks that I noticed a face in the foliage. Once I knew where it was, I could see it unmistakably every time I looked at it. I didn't tell my friends in case they thought I was deluded, but I did, I suppose accidentally, tell someone on the local paper, and they published a short piece on it. They didn't bother to send anybody around though. What made it interesting, I suppose, was that the face looked exactly like Mr. Bellini, the artist who had painted it."

"Mmmm," muttered Sam, "And of which garden is this … er, of. Is it yours?"

"Oh no, that's Mr. Bellini's garden. It's just around the corner, near where you parked your car." Sam winced. "Anthony's brother owns it now. He's pretty wealthy. He came over from Australia a few months before Anthony's death. After the funeral, he found lots and lots of Anthony's paintings in the attic – they're safely stored in a vault or somewhere now, of course – and I think he sells one whenever he finds he needs money." She laughed uncharacteristically and rather unpleasantly.

"Anyway, when he read about the face in the painting, he came right over. His name's Bertrand. He said he was fascinated to think that his brother's face might be hidden there, but he couldn't see it, and, when I looked, I couldn't see it either. And I've never been able to see it since. It was almost as if Anthony's brother's presence cancelled it out, almost like a double negative in mathematics, if I remember my schooldays correctly. I found it all rather confusing, which is why I called on you."

Sam thought that she was probably more concerned as to whether the painting had lost any of its original value.

Mrs. Dudley-Stewart continued, "Anyway, I called in an art expert, someone who knew a lot about Bellini's work, and he said it was definitely an authentic and genuine Anthony Bellini. He also said that Anthony never painted the same scene more than once. So, as the face disappeared months after Anthony's death, and the painting was in every other detail the same, it can't have been switched and I must have been imagining that face. And the ability to paint in a particular style is hardly hereditary, is it?"

If asked, Sam Diamond would have cheerfully admitted that he had absolutely no idea what was going on, but, if he didn't conclude the matter quickly, he felt sure that his client would terminate the case just as soon as his fees and expenses became marginally more than minimal, and he really needed some references and, more importantly, some money.

As far as Sam could see there was only one solution that fitted all the facts, or at least a few of them.

So he resolved to call on Mr. Bertrand Bellini as soon as possible.

Mr. Bellini looked a little surprised when Sam offered his private investigator's business card, but invited him into his lounge. He had a rather humorous or quizzical look on his face, as if he felt he were going to enjoy the meeting.

"Right, I shall come straight to the point, Sir," Sam said.

He then spent the next ten minutes doing anything but that, as he recounted his visit to Mrs. Dudley-Whatsit's house (he had already forgotten her full name, but he hoped he would have his memory jogged when she was writing out a cheque for him).

"So?" asked Mr. Bellini with one raised eyebrow. Sam hated that expression, purely because he had spent many hours in front of a mirror trying to do the same thing himself without success.

"I'm afraid I have rather an unpleasant accusation to make against you," he said pompously, trying to give the impression that he was or had until recently been in the police force. He had however seen an awful lot of detective films.

"And what might that be?" asked Mr. Bellini, his infuriating single eyebrow raised once more.

"Right. You come back from Australia. You see how well your brother, Anthony, is doing. You see all those paintings in the attic. You realise how much more they would be worth if he were deceased. So you give him an overdose, and leave him in the garden to die."

"I've already visited the local newspaper office, where I was able to confirm the way in which Anthony Bellini met his end."

"However, what you didn't know was that your brother had anticipated your attack, and had hidden evidence in his last painting, specifically to incriminate you. In fact, he must have died very close to where he painted his face in the painting."

Sam let his hands fall into his lap. He was pleased to see that both Mr. Bellini's eyebrows had shot up this time.

"And you have proof?" he asked.

"I don't think there'll be any problem there, not now that I've finally worked out what really happened. An exhumation should provide us with all the evidence needed." Sam tried to raise one eyebrow, but only succeeded in turning his rather unprepossessing visage into something even less aesthetic.

Mr. Bellini stood up and wandered around the room. He was clearly deep in thought. Sam thought to himself he would have a hard time explaining himself out of this one!

After a while, Mr. Bellini had clearly decided which approach to take. He cleared his throat.

"Right. You have presented a series of very well-reasoned and persuasive arguments for your case. I certainly find it difficult refuting what you have said …"

"So you confess?" said Sam, rather overexcitedly.

"Well, there are a few small pieces of evidence that perhaps you have overlooked, I'm sure accidentally …"

"Such as what?" demanded Sam.

Mr. Bellini started counting on his fingers.

"Well, firstly, I have a perfect and utterly-watertight alibi for the time – in fact, the whole day – of my brother's death."

Sam said nothing but thought, "Shit!"

"And secondly, the autopsy showed conclusively that my brother suffered from an advanced condition of cancer of the colon. You can check, but I can assure you that just about everybody around here knew that, including myself, so murdering him would be rather pointless."

"Thirdly, I assume that you're suggesting that I switched Mrs. Dudley-Stewart's painting for an almost perfectly identical picture, but without the face. As you say the current painting has been expertly authenticated as being by Anthony Bellini, how could I make the change so many months after his death?"

"Fourthly, if Anthony knew he was to be murdered, how could he know where he'd die, as depicted in the painting?"

"Fifthly, the paintings in storage …"

Sam was beginning to worry Mr. Bellini would run out of fingers, but he clearly decided to leave this one unsaid, and his voice trailed off.

"So I'm afraid, Mr. Detective, you're going to have to come up with a better theory than the one you've just propounded."

Sam said nothing, but tried to look intelligent.

After over two minutes of silence, Mr. Bellini again took up the conversation.

"Look, I think I can trust you, although I have absolutely no idea why. I think it's about time somebody else knew the truth, but I don't want it to go any further than this room. I shall certainly be able to compensate you more than adequately. And, as you'll soon realise, no real crime has been committed."

Sam spluttered, "I shall be the judge of that." Even by his standards he realised he sounded pompous.

"O.K. Can I talk in the third person, as if it were a story?"

After his last outburst, Sam nodded magnanimously.

"Bertrand had lived in Australia for many years. Doctors there had diagnosed he had cancer of the colon, so he returned here to spend his last few months, maybe days, with his brother, Anthony. He was hoping he might be helped with a planned suicide, as the pain was getting steadily worse, and he didn't think he would have the nerve to go through with that all on his own. Anthony was a bloody good painter, but he just wasn't selling much. One evening, over port,

Anthony suggested it would be better if he were to die instead. That would certainly push up the value of his paintings."

"That night, we decided to go ahead with the plan to switch bodies as it were."

"And I'm Anthony, if you hadn't realised by now."

Sam nodded nonchalantly as if he had known all along, but it was a poor attempt to hide his surprise.

"And so we just took it from there. We're brothers, not identical twins, but it didn't take too much effort to look similar. Although I hated Bertrand's lack of style, we switched the way we dressed. And Bertrand started attending a new dental clinic under my name."

"Anyway, an inquest showed the extent of the cancer, so suicide became all too likely. And my alibi was absolutely impeccable. I became Bertrand, and told people of the amazing number of paintings I had found in the attic. Of course, there weren't any. I just put a large number of blank canvases into secure storage, and withdrew one to paint on whenever I needed a little money."

"But I did feel a little uneasy about all this, I have to say."

"I'm not sure if it were consciously or subconsciously that, when I painted the garden just after my brother's arrival here and after we'd hatched the plan, I added his face. Then that dreadful Dudley woman started making it public in the local rag a short while after Anthony's death, so I decided it would have to go. I executed another painting, almost identical except for the face, called around, apparently out of interest and with some other paintings to show her, and switched the pictures. I didn't dream that she'd be so upset."

Bertrand, or rather Anthony, sat down and looked at Sam.

"So have we done anything morally wrong?"

Sam was just about to shake his head, when he remembered something, "So what's this remuneration for me?"

Anthony smiled.

"Well, I think it would calm the situation a little if that Dudley woman had the face back in her painting. So, if you'd like to take the original painting, which is in my attic, and switch it for hers, then you get her fee, small as I'm sure she'll insist it will be, she gets her painting with the face, and you get to keep the one I painted without the face. A genuine Anthony Bellini is worth quite a bit, I can assure you.."

Sam smiled.

Anthony added, "And you get the satisfaction of knowing that your reputation as a private investigator is assured."

Sam smiled again.

But he had already decided that, on the basis of his first case, he was going back to being a postman.

Chapter 7

Deep and Crisp and Evil

"With a bit of luck, we may be able to do a real bit of detective work here," mused Detective Inspector John Pratt.

His colleague, Constable Burbidge, looked blank, a look Pratt had for some time realised constituted his default expression.

The local police station had received a phone call at eight a.m. that morning to say that someone was very worried that something serious might have happened to old Mrs. Appleby. Her address was given, but the line went dead before the desk sergeant was able to ask for the caller's own details.

Less then thirty minutes later, the two policemen were standing outside a small bungalow on the outskirts of what used to be a thriving industrial area, but which now consisted almost solely of car parks and Grade II listed warehouses nobody could afford to maintain.

And the ground was liberally covered in snow.

"Look," Pratt explained, "We've just had a phone call to say something might have happened to the occupant. And the house is surrounded by snow! So, if there's been any sort of foul play, there may be footprints or some other clue. Yes? No?"

Burbidge nodded once, then a second time, more vigorously.

"It's eight thirty on a cold wintry Sunday morning, so no postman has been near the place." He looked along the street to where a paper-boy was starting to make deliveries at the other end of the street, "And no other deliveries seem to have been made yet either."

"So, as it started snowing around ten last night, and stopped around two this morning, if anyone has entered or left the house since two, then their footprints should be clearly visible. We should even see some imprint if anyone has been near the house after midnight, I would have thought."

"If anyone *has* committed a crime, that is," muttered Burbidge.

Pratt nodded distractedly. "Yes, you're right. Or else someone might have murdered the old dear and left the house before ten last night, and then phoned us this morning."

The house, adventurously but illiterately named "Chex Nous" according to a weather-beaten sign outside, was set within a fairly large plot, set well back from the walls that stood on all but the front side, where there was a low hedge. The rear wall was part of the back of a large windowless warehouse, and the two side walls were also high. No windows overlooked the property. Pratt looked carefully at the path from the front gate. There were clearly no signs of any footprints or other marks there or anywhere else on this side of the house.

They both reached the front door without finding anything suspicious at all. Pratt left Burbidge to wait there, and walked carefully around the house, looking for footprints or other clues. He couldn't see inside any of the windows, as all the curtains were drawn, and the only footprints he found were near Burbidge when he returned to the front door. He had been stamping his feet because of the cold.

Ringing the doorbell produced no reply, although they could see through the frosted window in the front door that there was a light shining from one of the back rooms off the hall.

"Try under the doormat," suggested Burbidge.

"Don't be daft," replied Pratt, "Nobody's stupid enough to do that these days."

"I do," said Burbidge, feeling under the mat and producing a door key.

Pratt accepted it ungratefully, and they moved into the hall.

All the doors in the hall were shut except for one. This was the last door on the right, at the end of the hall. The door was wide open and light spilled out into the hall. As it was at the rear of the building, it was probably a bedroom, thought Pratt.

But there was something that bothered Pratt.

"Wait at the front door," he said to Burbidge.

He was rewarded with the comment, "Why? If she's been murdered, she's not going to be running out of here, is she?"

Burbidge took up his post by the front door, striking a rather ridiculous pose. He clearly felt he was wasting his time, and was being kept away from all the excitement.

Pratt wandered down the hall and stopped at the entrance to the rear room, as if frozen.

An old lady, presumably Mrs. Appleby, was at the far corner of the room, sitting in a comfortable chair, although she didn't look that comfortable. She seemed dead, and a mug and a small plastic bottle on a table beside her both looked empty. It looked very much like the sort of tableau you might see in a waxworks or a museum.

Even if everything did look so right in the little well-lit room, Pratt still had that niggling worry.

He walked over to the old lady. She was indeed dead, and looked as if she had been dead for some time, perhaps since midnight. It looked as if she'd taken an overdose of pills. The empty bottle beside her indicated that it had once contained tablets she had very recently been prescribed.

Pratt thought deeply, something he had felt unable to do when Burbidge had been standing beside him. Burbidge had a habit of making strange noises with his mouth as if he were continually trying to floss his teeth with his tongue.

No, something was definitely wrong.

It worried him a little that he seemed to have been intended to be drawn as far away from the front door as possible. All the other doors were shut, but this bedroom door was open, the light was on, and the old lady was seated in the corner furthest away from the door. But that could be coincidence.

It also seemed odd that the old lady should be indoors, and yet the key had been left under the mat. Suicides were sometimes very considerate though, and she might not have wanted what was to be her heir's property to be damaged if a forced entry were to be made.

But there was something else, something more important ...

Yes, of course! How could anyone have known to notify the police at eight in the morning that they were worried about Mrs. Appleby if there were no footprints around the house, and no way of looking into any of the rooms? Either they had known something was wrong before it snowed, in which case why did they wait until so late in the morning before phoning, or ...

He went back into the hall and called to Burbidge to stay where he was whatever happened.

He checked the kitchen, the other bedroom, and the lounge. They were all empty.

Suddenly, there was a crash and loud voices. A youth had run out of the bathroom and was fighting with Burbidge.

The lad ran back into the bathroom.

Pratt now engaged him in a brief fight, the youth repeatedly trying to stab him with a dried loofah, but, eventually, the lad was subdued after Burbidge disobeyed instructions, and left his post and joined the fight.

The youth's name was Barry Appleby.

There was very little point in Barry's not confessing everything. If the two policemen had rushed straight to the body in the well-lit room, instead of John Pratt's realising that something was wrong and making sure someone was stationed at the front door, Barry would have escaped, mixed up his footprints with those already in the snow, and probably got away with it by denying any accusations that might be made.

Barry had intended staying the previous night at his girlfriend's, where he had been resident for the last few months. He hadn't got a job or anywhere of his own to live, and so had had to find some girl with a house or a flat.

She had finally tired of him and the way he was obviously using her, and had kicked him out the previous afternoon. He thought he would have to sleep in his old Ford Capri, but then decided to pay a visit to his Gran. Perhaps she would give him some money, he thought, although all his begging had fallen on deaf ears ever since he had passed the age of ten.

She was as unyielding as she usually was, but she agreed that he could stay the night, "Just the one, mind you."

He vanished to the bathroom for a while, sat down, and thought.

When he finally emerged, he had decided to pour an overdose of her tablets into her nightcap. He was sure he was one of only two beneficiaries, and the house must have been worth quite a bit.

She drank her cocoa at ten o'clock. Then he settled down on her spare bed for a few hours to await the outcome.

He was never an early riser, but this Sunday he was excited. He rose at six, checked that she was definitely dead, and then set everything up to look like a suicide, including removing any indication that anyone had spent the night there.

He always called in for a free Sunday lunch at his grandmother's, but he didn't want to be the one to discover her body. Anyway, the sooner she were found, the more likely he felt he would be able to suggest that he had been somewhere else. So he decided to telephone the police. That way, he wouldn't have to find the body and could suggest he had been asleep in his car all night.

When everything was ready, he made the phone call and headed for the front door to leave. He wanted to register his presence away from the house as soon as possible.

Then he saw the snow all around.

That must have been quite a shock for him.

If he left the house then, the police would probably spot his footprints and might then suspect that Mrs. Appleby had been murdered, rather than taken her own life. The prints might even provide forensic evidence to connect him with her death.

He had tried to think clearly. He arranged the house so that anybody entering would be drawn towards the room furthest from the front door. He left the key under the mat, as he didn't want attention drawn to the house by two burly policemen breaking down the door, and witnesses spotting him as he made his escape. He hoped that all this would give him the chance to escape from the bathroom at the front of the house without being seen. After a couple of flat-footed policemen had been wandering around the garden, he felt sure his footprints would be undetectable.

But now he wouldn't need to worry about somewhere to stay the night for a considerable number of years.

Chapter 8

RIP

Even Detective Inspector Cecil Biedermeyer himself would have been the first to acknowledge that he would never have been put in charge of such a potentially high-profile murder investigation had it not been for the fact that every other detective in the force was heavily involved in security and other matters relating to the imminent Royal Wedding. Although Prince Joseph and his intended, Justine Courtenay, were both very popular with the majority of the public, there had been a number of threats from odd and rather vague sources. The anti-monarchists were naturally voicing protests against just about every aspect of the ceremony, but even some of those who supported the Royal Family were protesting that the bride-to-be was from an insufficiently-aristocratic lineage. Security was at the highest level for decades, even though the date was still some months away.

Cecil Biedermeyer had always managed to keep his level of competence just above the absolute minimum required. He had been in charge of a few fairly-important cases at the start of his career, but none since, for reasons that even he was willing to accept. He had tried, fairly convincingly, to look the part. He had a bald domed head and a short moustache similar to that adopted by Adolf Hitler (although his demeanour meant that nobody ever thought of Hitler when they met him), and he habitually wore a long beige trench coat he had seen some police inspector wearing in a 1950s British B-movie. However, none of this worked, except from the theatrical point of view.

That he should have been placed in charge of a murder investigation at all was quite a shock to anyone who knew him even slightly.

A young, smartly-dressed girl had been found bizarrely and brutally murdered in a street in East London. Cecil was a little perturbed that, for such a potentially high-profile crime, he had been assigned only one police constable for support, but hoped that he could soon overemphasise the case's importance, and either have more assistance, or, better still, have someone take over the case from him. If he couldn't get a scapegoat, his best chance was to pass the buck. He felt pretty sure that he was going to need considerable help though, as he was beginning to feel that this was more than a little out of the normal run of things. Although he was rarely involved with detection - or rather, successful detection - in the real world, he was an avid reader of detective fiction and stories of real-life murders, and the initial few sketchy details about this murder had an ominous ring to them.

He turned the car into Durward Street, and was surprised at the amount of activity there. The assistant that he had been assigned was P.C. Brighouse, who was waiting for him in part of a large area that had been cordoned off.

"It looks as if Jack the Ripper's back in business, Sir," he said smiling.

"This is hardly a matter to be taken flippantly, Brighouse. What have you got?"

"She's Melanie Amber Northwood. Her apartment is in Snowdon Court, a very expensive area, I can assure you. She's had her throat cut, not too savagely, but enough to do the job. She's also been gashed along the abdomen, but that's only a little cut, and not the cause of death. The doctor is pretty sure she was murdered elsewhere and then dumped here."

"Mmm," Detective Inspector Biedermeyer looked at the corpse. "It's not Jack the Ripper's style really, is it? He would hardly have been so half-hearted about it, and he only seemed to murder prostitutes and women of that sort. This one seems to be fairly upper-class and well-off, judging from her clothing. My wife could only dream of being able to afford clothes like that."

"Nevertheless," continued Brighouse, whose Christian name was Harold, not that anyone ever used that, "She *was* a prostitute. Very high-class, I'll admit. I used to patrol around where she lived, and I can assure you that's her profession. She only had a few customers then - they paid a lot for semi-exclusive access - and she may have had only a single client recently. That's what they all seem to want to aim for these days."

Cecil felt he didn't need to bother the police doctor with questions at that stage, as Brighouse seemed to have condensed all the necessary medical details into his verbal report. He had also checked for witnesses, but had failed to unearth any evidence in that respect.

Cecil's stomach was beginning to play up as it often did, so he decided he'd better return home.

"Got her address, lad?" he enquired.

"Well, there's no address in her handbag, but I know roughly where she lived. I can check with the others in the block as to the actual number. It'll probably have to be a forced entry though, as there's no key on her."

"O.K. Do that. I've got some research to do. Phone my mobile and let me know how you get on."

Cecil's mobile rang.

"Sir? I managed to get into her apartment. It's been ransacked, neatly though. There doesn't seem to be any evidence that Melanie was killed there, but Forensics are still looking."

"Oh, and it looks as if she did have only one client, Sir." He named a millionaire industrialist. "But there are plenty of photos of him around, so it doesn't look as if he's the killer. It could be a double bluff, I suppose."

Cecil grunted, "Or else another client removed all the photographs he himself was in. Are there no other names?"

"There aren't many. There are a few letters from relatives, but no names who might be clients. Her address book's gone, if she ever had one, but I've unearthed the names and addresses of two, er, colleagues, shall we say. I'll check up on those tomorrow, if you like, Sir."

Cecil nodded pointlessly, and then thought for a while. "It's hardly a random killing by someone who hates prostitutes if the killer went and searched her apartment. Anyway, she didn't look like a prostitute. It's either her client, who has kindly left his photos all over the place, another client who had the sense to remove his, or a friend or colleague."

"Anyway, I've got work to do," he muttered, switching off the phone.

Oddly enough, Cecil Biedermeyer really did have some work to do. He was a little alarmed that there seemed to be so many parallels with Jack the Ripper.

He know he had a book somewhere with all the details, and spent the best part of an hour trying to find it. Eventually he found it among his holiday photograph albums.

Exactly how many victims Jack had killed nobody seemed sure. The number seemed to change with each new book published. In Cecil's fairly old book, the first victim had been Mary Ann Nichols, a domestic servant and casual prostitute in her forties, who had been found in Buck's Row, Whitechapel, on Friday, August the thirty-first, 1888. Her head had been almost cut off and there were large gashes along her abdomen.

Cecil sat back, deep in thought.

Well, Melanie's injuries were similar, although rather more half-hearted than Jack's original frenzied slashing. The initials were the same. But the day was different - it was Thursday today - and this was September, not August. Or was it? Oh God, it was September the first tomorrow, so the date matched too. Where was Buck's Row? He got out a set of London street maps, but he couldn't find it.

But he knew the answer even before he phoned up one of those operators of sensationally gory walking tours of London. They confirmed that they did indeed run one which visited the sites of Jack's murders.

And yes, Buck's Row approximated to present-day Durward Street.

He sat back. Now he had something with which to convince his superior to give him more staff, or, better still, to give the investigation to someone more competent.

"It's clear someone has decided to take on Jack the Ripper's mantle and start culling prostitutes in Whitechapel again, Sir. This is getting important. I'm sure the media will start focusing on it soon, and that could seriously harm tourism. Don't forget we have thousands of foreigners about to flood into London for the Royal Wedding."

"I think you're overreacting, Cecil," was his superior's verdict. "It's just a one-off. Someone had a personal grudge against the girl - perhaps she was blackmailing one of her clients - and he decided to tidy things up a bit. He must have decided to copy Jack the Ripper in order to confuse matters."

"Just get on with it. I'd like this sorted out as soon as possible."

So Detective Inspector Cecil Biedermeyer was still in the hot seat, as he liked to put it.

He had left Brighouse to do all the footwork, but he had come up with next to nothing. No further clues had come to light, and the two colleagues whose addresses had been found had not been particularly forthcoming. It seemed that prostitutes were rather tight-lipped when talking to the police.

He wondered whether there might be some clue to be found in the details of the original crimes.

There hadn't been that large a number of obvious suspects for the previous set of gruesome murders. It was clear that whoever had been responsible had had a pretty good knowledge of surgery and anatomy, something that few people then would have possessed. People today were better-educated and better-informed, and had access to much more extensive sources of information.

The press, the public and the police had all considered local doctors, nurses and midwives, together with less-qualified medical practitioners and back-street abortionists (with whom many of the victims would have been acquainted). People from other countries were a particularly popular choice. So were those who were well-educated and respectable, as they might have had more idea about medical matters and a greater access to the necessary information. Even royalty was suspected by some. He wondered whether Prince Joseph could be considered a suspect in this current investigation. He realised he was thinking at random and not using the powers of deduction he was supposed to possess.

But things continued in the same vein for over a week. Brighouse unearthed nothing new of interest, and Cecil continued to practise ratiocination unsuccessfully, although this was largely in order to think of something new to present to his boss to get his workload shifted.

Then Cecil Biedermeyer realised that it was September the eighth, exactly eight days after the murder of Melanie Amber Northwood.

He and Brighouse had already considered the possibility that, if this were a series of Jack the Ripper copycat murders, the next one might be scheduled for today. He checked his Jack the Ripper book again. Annie Chapman, a 47-year-old with a number of jobs including that of casual prostitute, had been found in the backyard of 29 Hanbury Street in the early hours of Saturday, September the eighth, 1888. Her injuries had been similar to those inflicted on Mary Ann Nichols, but rather more gruesome. Her intestines had been placed on her shoulders, and her uterus was never found.

He checked his map for Hanbury Street and was luckier this time. It still existed, and he made arrangements to pick up Brighouse on the way.

It was a sign of the esteem in which Cecil Biedermeyer was held by the force that he was always assigned the oldest and least-reliable car in the pool. Today was no exception, and ten a.m. found him and Brighouse stranded by the side of the Thames. The radio didn't work either, so it was some time before they reached Hanbury Street.

Jayne-Michelle Knight was already there in a few black plastic dustbin bags.

Now Cecil Biedermeyer really had something to twist his boss's arm.

There was clearly a serial killer on the loose, repeating the trail of carnage that Jack the Ripper had laid in the nineteenth century.

This time, the initials were different, not that that seemed important, but the day and place were the same, and the injuries similar. Jayne-Michelle had been subjected to similar knife wounds to those of her predecessor, but thankfully her innards hadn't been extracted and everything that should be inside her still was. She also appeared to have been killed elsewhere and dumped in Hanbury Street.

"You're right, Cecil," agreed his superior, "It looks as if we could have trouble from the Press on this one. No-one likes the thought of a knife-wielding lunatic making the streets of London unsafe for others at night." Cecil wondered just how out of touch with modern life his boss was.

"You've made your point very well. I'm impressed," continued his boss.

Cecil was assigned the full-time services of a PR and media advisor.

Jayne-Michelle's address had been more difficult to trace this time. Her flat had also been ransacked carefully and efficiently. Again, there was evidence of her clientele, two men this time, and some addresses of friends and colleagues, but no obvious link with Melanie Amber Northwood, apart from the fact that they were both high-class prostitutes. There seemed to be no friends that they shared, and there was no evidence that they had ever met or had even known of each other's existence.

Even if they been chosen at random to satisfy someone's macabre blood-lust, it would have had to have been someone who knew their backgrounds and current 'occupation,' which was certainly nowhere near as obvious as it was for Jack the Ripper in his day.

But there had to be *some* common link.

Whilst Cecil mostly sat in the office and theorised, Brighouse did almost all the legwork, interviewing and sometimes re-interviewing friends and acquaintances of the two deceased girls. He also tried to interview any other co-workers in the area, but this was difficult, as these high-class prostitutes didn't need to advertise, as it were, and they tended to be particularly difficult to find. Even Cecil had had to conduct some of the interviews himself, in particular whenever the interviewee was one of the more important clients and things had to be handled diplomatically, although whether his abilities were any better-suited for this was open to question.

But their investigations did not progress far. Little evidence had been found, and no arrest was imminent. It looked as if Cecil might have to await further developments.

He had already guessed what these would be.

The phone rang. It was Brighouse.

"Look, Sir, have you considered that maybe the real victim hasn't been killed yet? Perhaps someone is intending to kill a particular prostitute, but is making the motive unclear by murdering a number of other prostitutes first."

"Eh?" said Cecil blankly.

"As in Christie, Sir," explained Brighouse.

"Ah, 10 Rillington Place," muttered Cecil, thinking he was beginning to understand.

"No, Sir, Agatha Christie. She wrote a novel in which each murder victim seemed to be part of a sequence taken in order. Everyone was convinced that the murderer had some sort of lethal preoccupation with that sequence. But in fact there was only one of these victims that the murderer really wanted to kill, and the others were merely to hide the motive. Couldn't our two murders be part of a series of murders, all of prostitutes, paralleling the career of Jack the Ripper, but only one of which would be directly to the murderer's benefit?"

"It isn't likely, lad, is it?" Cecil said, trying to finish the conversation.

Brighouse clearly hadn't finished.

"Anyway, the next one's due on September the thirtieth, Sir, and this time there are two of them."

Not that Cecil Biedermeyer hadn't already worked that out.

On that date in 1888, Elizabeth Stride, a 44-year-old Swedish prostitute known as 'Long Liz,' had been killed in a yard off Berner Street, now renamed Henriques Street. Her body had still been warm and bleeding when found, and was not as mutilated as the others. Jack had clearly been interrupted, but his blood-lust had been satisfied by a second killing that night. Catherine Eddowes, 46, had been killed in Mitre Square, Aldgate, and had been savagely attacked.

"Keep working at it, lad," he advised. "With a bit of luck, we'll find something before then."

But neither of them did. And it was now the morning of September the thirtieth.

The phone rang on Cecil Biedermeyer's tidy and nigh-empty desk.

"Yes, Brighouse," he answered, "Have you got anything?"

Surprisingly, it wasn't Brighouse.

"Mr. Biedermeyer?" asked the caller politely. He nodded.

"Mr Cecil Biedermeyer?" continued the voice on the other end of the phone.

"How many ruddy Biedermeyers do you think we've got here?" Cecil almost screamed down the phone.

The voice seemed undeterred. It was female, very refined and elegant, and with a very slight West Country burr to it.

"I rather thought you would have caught the Ripper by now," it continued. "I have been reading the press and searching through reference books about the original Jack, and there are two due today you realise."

Cecil replied that he knew that only too ruddy well.

The soft voice continued, "Well, I think I may very well be one of the next victims."

Cecil thought for a second. Normally, he would have been very cautious about this. He was by nature the sort of person who doesn't jump to conclusions or take things at face value, perhaps as a by-product of being work-shy, but in this instance he was prepared to take any evidence that anyone cared to present to him.

"And so you need police protection of course. I'll get some men around to you in a few minutes. Where do you live?"

"My name is Lavinia Blythe-Gordon, and I live at Apartment 47 in Heathcote Towers. I think I'd like you to be here as soon as possible."

Cecil Biedermeyer nodded his agreement. He wasn't quite sure why he did that when he was on the phone. He knew where Heathcote Towers was. "We'll be there within minutes."

It was only as he put down the phone that he realised he hadn't asked who Lavinia suspected of plotting her demise. Neither had he taken her telephone number. But, he reasoned, speed was of the essence.

Heathcote Towers was in a quiet corner of Mayfair.

Brighouse had been telephoned from Biedermeyer's car. After the debacle on the day of the second murder, Biedermeyer's car was now one of the best the force could offer. This was clearly an indication of the rising public profile of the case.

They arrived at the foyer together. Even with their official identification, it took some time to get past the concierge. That the apartments were expensive was demonstrated by the fact that the first lift they tried worked.

The door to Apartment 47 was slightly ajar.

Lavinia Blythe-Gordon's murder was different to its nineteenth-century predecessor in so far as it was discovered indoors, it was in a totally different location, and it had taken place mid-morning. However, both bore the hallmarks of extreme haste.

Lavinia's throat had been cut, but there were no other visible injuries. The apartment had been more cursorily ransacked than on the other two occasions. Only a few drawers had been left open and their contents strewn around.

"We're a bit late," said Cecil sadly, and perhaps a little unnecessarily.

Brighouse nodded. "Jack's obviously just left, though. He may have left behind something interesting this time."

Not much, but something. It was photograph of Lavinia, Jayne-Michelle Knight, and two friends, neither of whom they recognised. Brighouse found it hidden in a drawer, placed neatly between folded underwear. "It's the first place I look," he explained, or rather half-explained.

And that was all.

"O.K., lad. Get copies made, and circulate it to anyone you can find in the same line of business. I want to know who those other two are."

Cecil Biedermeyer knew he had made a grave error in not asking his caller more questions, but resolved to do better the next time it happened.

Although this third killing had not copied the original murder as closely as the others, the two policemen were still expecting the fourth to take place that day.

The number of policemen on foot in the Aldgate area, especially around Mitre Square, was increased dramatically. Any cars in the area were asked to look out for any suspicious activity. Unfortunately, no further resources were available.

The two policemen resolved to meet at lunchtime at Cecil's small flat, before moving on to Aldgate.

"I doubt we can prevent the murder today, as we don't know where it will be taking place, but we know where the body should finish up, and so we may be able to catch Jack red-handed."

Brighouse nodded. "Jack's clever though. He'll be expecting that, and he'll try and find some way of fooling us."

"Mmm," commented Cecil, coming back from the kitchen corner with two steaming mugs of coffee. Brighouse had been staring at the only real bit of evidence they had - Lavinia's photograph.

He tapped it gently. "There's more to this than one might think, you know. Why did Lavinia hide it so carefully? Was she expecting someone to call, someone who would want to take away or destroy the photograph?"

He started playing around with it, covering various parts of the photograph with his hands.

"Can I write on it?" he suddenly asked.

"No you cannot, lad. That's the original. But I've got a scanner with my P.C. in the attic"

They clambered up a small ladder into the attic, which was just a small area under the roof where anything not needed on a daily basis was stored.

The photograph was put into the scanner, and a few copies were printed off from the computer.

Brighouse grabbed a pencil and started darkening the blonde hair of one of Lavinia's friends in the photograph.

He smiled and handed it over to his boss. A well-known face looked back at them.

"Trying to cover up her past," muttered Cecil.

"Now we know, we shouldn't have much problem tracing her movements for the past few weeks. After all, she's been under almost-constant surveillance and protection."

"She needs protection?" enquired Brighouse cheekily.

Suddenly, it became quite cold in the attic. Cecil shivered. "I'd better go down and phone my boss," he said.

The coffee was at least still warm. They both had a long drink while sifting over the evidence and facts in their minds.

Brighouse was the first to break the silence.

"I've always thought of you as a bit of a connoisseur of coffee, Sir. But isn't there chicory in this?"

It did taste bitter, Cecil had to agree. He picked up his phone and began to dial his boss. Brighouse started to vomit copiously. He slumped to the floor. He stopped moving. And breathing.

Cecil's boss's wife answered the phone.

"Get me your husband, quickly," he pleaded, "This is an emergency."

She thankfully caught the urgency in his voice and didn't reprimand him for curtness. "Well, he's in the greenhouse at the moment, and I normally wouldn't disturb him when he's with his lobelias, but, under the circumstances ..."

He heard her retreating footsteps over the phone and waited for what seemed to be an eternity. His stomach started to feel as bad as it had after he had visited a notorious Indian restaurant as a result of a bet with his colleagues. Eventually, his boss came to the phone.

"What's this all ..." he thundered, less sympathetically than his wife.

"We know who the Ripper is, Sir," Cecil interrupted him. "It's Justine ..."

Or so he thought he said. Instead, his voice trailed off into nothing after his first eight words.

Cecil Biedermeyer pivoted slowly on his heel and crashed headlong to the wine-red floor.

Chapter 9

The First of Criminals

Jeannine Forrest was sitting in front of the television with a ghastly expression on her face.

The television was showing a late-night screening of an old Shirley Temple film, but that wasn't the cause of Jeannine's expression.

That she had been strangled was evident from the marks on her neck. The doctor was still examining her.

While he was busy with his examination, D.I. John Pratt looked around the room.

Jeannine's house, or rather her parents' house, was a small terraced house in a "good area" of Gammonham. D.I. Pratt wondered whether Jeannine's parents preferred a "good address" to a suitably large house, as Jeannine had had four brothers and sisters. These had now left home to live on their own, and so it had been Mum and Dad who had discovered Jeannine when they came back from a visit to some local function around eleven.

The decor was what Pratt would have described as 'good-class kitsch.' It looked as if the Forrests had some idea of what style was, but didn't have the money to back it up. There wasn't anything in the room as expensive as it was meant to look. All the electrical equipment on display (and there was plenty of it in the lounge) was either exceptionally large or exceptionally small, depending on what was deemed the more appropriate for that particular item. However, all were marked with names that seemed to be anagrams or misspelled versions of those of the better-known manufacturers. The television had a screen that seemed larger than those in the flea-pit cinemas he had habitually visited as a small child, and was manufactured by the Sany Corporation, whilst the mobile phones - there were three of them in evidence - were made by Nukia, and would have been useless to anyone with normally-sized fingers. There was a 1960's-style Astro lamp on a small coffee table alongside some trendy but unreadable (and clearly unread) coffee-table books. Pratt touched the lamp, and, even though it was nigh red-hot, the 'lava' had stayed resolutely at the bottom and had failed to rise.

"I'll give you more details later," Dr. Latham said, standing up. "Time of death: probably around eight thirty to ten thirty. Cause: well, you can see for yourself. I'll have more information around two p.m. tomorrow." Dr. Latham had that unfortunate combination of being bald but still having dandruff. As usual, he was in a hurry, and left through the door in an apparent snow-storm.

The case should be nice and simple anyway, thought Pratt. It was obviously not a bungled burglary, and Jeannine's parents confirmed she had had two boyfriends, one incoming, one outgoing, and that was that in terms of the number of suspects.

Next morning, D.I. Pratt arrived outside Derek James' house. Both boyfriends lived only a short distance from Jeannine's house. Derek was apparently the 'outgoing' boyfriend.

"Jeannine and I had been going out together for quite a few years. Childhood sweethearts I suppose we were, but we sort of split up recently. I think Jeannine was rather surprised and flattered that someone like John Tyrwhit would have been interested in her. I mean, she was good looking, but hardly in the same social class as Tyrwhit. His family are pretty well-off and have a lot of social standing. The name is supposed to be one of the oldest in the county, or so she said he told her. I don't think Mr. and Mrs. Forrest actually disapproved of me, but they made it clear that they would have preferred her to be married to someone they thought more eligible. And there would be few people more eligible than Tyrwhit. I'm sure they encouraged her to accept Tyrwhit's advances. I wasn't able to compete with that."

He half-smiled. "But anyway, she telephoned me yesterday evening, and said she wanted to start going out with me again. I don't know whether Tyrwhit had dumped her, or whether she had decided she wanted me instead. I never saw her again to discuss it."

Not that he had any proof of that, Pratt thought. He said he had been in the house all evening on his own. His parents had attended the same civic function as Jeannine's parents had.

The next visit was to the Tyrwhit residence.

Unlike the other two houses he had visited, Barrington Manse was a large detached house of considerable charm. It was set well back from the main road towards Barrington, and looked like the sort of house that might have been built for the local rector in the middle of the nineteenth century.

D.I. Pratt was sitting in his car admiring the architecture of the house when his mobile phone rang.

"Hello, Latham here. I've got a full written report for you, er ..." he could be heard rummaging through a large pile of papers, "... somewhere, but, in the meantime, you might like to know that she wasn't sexually assaulted in any way, that death was due to strangulation, and she died between eight and nine thirty."

"Definitely?" asked Pratt.

"Definitely. My written report will be with you as soon as I can locate it," Latham replied, finishing the conversation abruptly as his phone fell from its place between his chin and his shoulder.

Pratt sat in his car for a while longer, thinking, and excavating his auditory orifice with his finger. Then he got out and headed for the house.

Despite a considerable number of expensive, but not ostentatious, vehicles in the large drive (and a nearby coach house may well have been similarly stocked), John Tyrwhit appeared to be in the house on his own. He opened the door to D.I. Pratt, and invited him into the great hall.

The interior of the house was tastefully redolent of an earlier age. Everything seemed fitting. It was obvious that the atmosphere was authentic, and not merely acquired from some antiques emporium.

On the wall, there was an impressive document charting the family tree, carefully kept up-to-date, judging by some clearly recent annotations, and a family crest over the fireplace with what Pratt was pleased to note was a family motto in Latin that was really rather rude. His Latin O-level had at last paid off.

John Tyrwhit motioned D.I. Pratt into an uncomfortable and unyielding, but obviously ancient, seat near the fireplace. "Dreadful news. I'm sorry I don't show grief very well. I suppose coming from my sort of background, one's taught to hide it. I do feel absolutely terrible inside, though."

Pratt mumbled a reply, and asked about Tyrwhit's recent activities.

"Yesterday evening? Some of my colleagues at University had hired a minibus to go to Wilchester for a match. They dropped me off at the end of this road at 9.45 p.m. The others weren't that inebriated, well, the driver wasn't very drunk anyway, so they should be able to confirm all this. I got home at 9.55 p.m., so I don't think I can be considered a suspect."

"How long have you known Jeannine?" Pratt asked.

"Well, I've known her for quite a while, but we've only been going out for, well, less than a week I suppose, but it seems as if we've been together for years."

Outside in his car again, D.I. Pratt sat musing. Now he had two suspects, both with possible motives, but only one with a good enough alibi for all of the period between eight and nine thirty.

Tyrwhit must be in the clear. Pratt had telephoned Tyrwhit's house early that morning, and, finding him to be out, had chatted briefly to his father. Having been told that he had been on a trip to Wilchester, he had got as many details as possible. One of his subordinates had contacted most of his fellow-passengers on the minibus, as well as some of those they had visited at Wilchester, and they had all fully verified Tyrwhit's story.

So he only had one suspect now.

Unfortunately, he found himself warming to Derek James, and disapproving of John Tyrwhit and finding his manner hard to like. He hadn't realised how much his working-class background influenced his attitudes towards others. He resolved to try and overcome it ... and yet ...

Normally, he would have gone straight around to Derek James' house and started putting the pressure on. But he decided he'd stay in the car and think a little more.

But there was some niggling little thought at the back of his mind. He thought a bit more. What was worrying him?

Yes, of course! Why had Tyrwhit assumed he was in the clear when Pratt himself had only just learnt that Latham had finalised his assessment of the time of death, revising his earlier estimate?

He knocked again on the door of Barrington Manse.

John Tyrwhit looked surprised to see him again so quickly.

D.I. Pratt, who was wearing his usual shabby outfit anyway, put his hand to his brow in his best impression of television's Columbo. "There was just one more thing," he muttered. "I like to get a feel for the background of any case I'm involved in. Have you any objection to my having a look around the great hall? There seems to be a great feeling of tradition here, and I think it might explain why Jeannine felt her future lay in this environment rather than with Derek James."

"It's all yours," welcomed Tyrwhit, waving expansively. However, he still stayed fairly close, probably to ensure that no heirlooms were stolen.

D.I. Pratt began to look around the hall in a vague and general way, but then moved purposefully towards the splendid family tree he had seen earlier.

"Yes!" he suddenly yelled, punching the air triumphantly. Tyrwhit looked visibly shocked at the change in his demeanour.

"But he knows," thought Pratt.

And so did D.I. Pratt. He had to get a second, and, to make absolutely certain, a third opinion on the time of death of Jeannine Forrest.

Doctor Latham had been right first time. Jeannine had died between 8.30 p.m. and 10.30 p.m., and Tyrwhit had killed her when he had called around after the trip to Wilchester. There had been an argument when she said she was going back to Derek. He probably hadn't wanted to lose face.

The family tree had included a marriage between Reginald Tyrwhit and a member of the Latham family a few decades earlier.

D.I. Pratt smiled uncharacteristically. He had very little more work to do … that is, as long as the two other doctors' reports tallied with Doctor Latham's original estimate of the time of death, which had obviously been made before the Doctor knew of John Tyrwhit's involvement.

And they did.

He thought of a quotation from Conan Doyle's 'The Adventure of the Speckled Band.'

"When a doctor does go wrong he is the first of criminals. He has nerve and he has knowledge."

Chapter 10

The Final Proof

D.I. John Pratt knew instinctively that Mrs. Martin had been poisoned.

Which was unusual, as he was most definitely not the sort of policeman who acted instinctively. He always worked methodically through the evidence, invariably collecting far more than was needed, and only made an arrest when the accused's guilt was absolutely beyond doubt. In theory, this made him an utterly dependable and fair member of the police force, but, in reality, it meant that he made fewer arrests than most of his colleagues. Early in his career, he had been known as Plod, he hoped affectionately.

It was a neighbour who had called the police. Mrs. Watkins habitually called around to Mrs. Martin's for "a cup of tea and a chat" at 11.00 a.m. on Tuesdays. This Tuesday, nobody answered the door, and so she peered through the blinds of each of the downstairs windows (D.I. Pratt thought that this was probably a physical version of the sort of chat they would have had). Mrs. Martin was eventually glimpsed sitting "unnaturally" at the small table in the middle of the kitchen, obviating the need for Mrs. Watkins to go and get a ladder and some binoculars. Mrs. Watkins called the police immediately (she said she thought it best not to telephone Mr. Martin first, as "she knew there had been some turbulence in their marriage of late").

The police, however, did telephone Mr. Martin at his office, if only to avoid a forced entry.

The scene that confronted D.I. Pratt as he and Mr. Martin entered the kitchen seemed serene and relaxed. Mrs. Martin was sitting, unmoving, at the table, a pot of tea and an empty tea-cup in front of her. But, for some reason, Pratt immediately "knew" that she had been poisoned. Perhaps it was the very serenity there that suggested it to him. The rest of the room (and indeed the whole house) was very neat and well-ordered, and even the presence of Mrs. Martin's body failed to suggest any degree of untidiness.

D.I. Pratt didn't think he'd be able to find anything of any interest there ... only Forensics would. He made sure that nobody, especially Mr. Martin, went anywhere near the body or any of the items on the table, and arranged for a report to be sent to him as soon as any medical information was available ... and he knew what that information would be even before Forensics did.

Whilst Mr. Martin went off for a recommended rest at his brother's, Pratt decided to pay a visit to his place of work.

"It's purely an informal visit," D.I. Pratt said. "We're sure Mr. Martin's wife died of natural causes, but we like to get some of the background details." However, he had his fingers crossed inside his pocket, next to his mobile phone, which he expected to ring at any moment with news about Mrs. Martin's cause of death.

Mr. Martin worked as one of three readers at a small literary agency in Aleford, Sheila Wilson-Black. D.I. Pratt had already asked to speak with Miss Wilson-Black, but apparently she had never existed, and so he was shown into the office of the owner and manager, Harry Black (with no Wilson or hyphen).

"What exactly do you, and particularly Mr. Martin, do here?" asked Pratt bluntly.

"Well, people who have written a book and want to see it in print contact us for our opinion and help in getting it published. They make a preliminary enquiry, and, if we're interested, we ask them to send us a sample of their oeuvre. If we're *still* interested, they send us the whole novel or whatever. Then we read it, suggest changes or give assistance in some other way, and then submit it to a publisher for consideration. Publishers very rarely deal directly with authors these days, you know. We normally deal with romantic fiction and science fantasy."

Pratt mused, "What would Martin have been working on recently? Er, science fantasy?" He felt sure that romantic fiction was not his interest.

"That's what he mainly deals with, yes. I'll check." Harry Black got out a file from a cupboard. "Yes, he's currently reading a number of novels and a few sample chapters - all science fiction and that sort of stuff."

The mobile phone rang in Pratt's pocket. He answered it.

He was pleased to hear that a preliminary report on Mrs. Martin was now available.

He was not pleased to hear that she must have died from natural causes, although these were as yet unknown.

He excused himself, and wandered into the hallway outside the office.

"There were no traces of poison or anything like that?" he whispered.

It was his assistant on the other end of the line. He had anticipated all Pratt's questions. "No poison or anything like that. There was nothing unusual at all about her death, it seems. Her doctor has confirmed that there was hardly anything wrong with her, only a very, very slight heart murmur, that's all. She didn't need to take any medication. In short, there was nothing suspicious at all, and it should only be a matter of time before they diagnose to what natural causes to attribute her death."

"Sorry, Sir," he added.

Pratt returned to Harry Black's office to continue his conversation, even though he could hardly justify it now. He still thought Mrs. Martin must have been murdered, and didn't like her husband anyway. Especially now.

"Did Martin ever handle detective fiction?" he asked.

"Very occasionally, but not recently. The last book of that sort he read has just gone into print actually, so it was probably around a year ago that he was first asked to review it."

A thought came into Pratt's head. "I don't suppose it ever happens that someone submits a book, and then, before publication, dies or leaves the country. Does that ever happen?"

"It does, but rarely, and certainly not within the last few years or so, as I'd remember it. Anyway, if the author passed away, the publishers might not be too keen to proceed with the book, as there would be no chance of a sequel if it were successful."

"Mmm," said Pratt thoughtfully. He found he couldn't think of anything else to ask, and so added finally, "You couldn't give me the name and address of the author of that detective book that Mr. Martin read, could you?"

Harry Black said yes, and handed over a file so that he could note the details. He didn't know why, though.

Even an autopsy could still not pinpoint the cause of death. It was finally decided it must have been some problem with her heart.

D.I. Pratt was not happy. This was mainly because he had, for once, told most of his department of his theory about the death, that he was convinced it would be found to be murder, also certainly a poison.

He took a week off. He said he needed a rest, but it was mainly because he couldn't face those in his office for a while.

His local travel agency was unable to offer any of the stupendously cheap last-minute offers that all his retired friends seemed able to book. So he found himself wandering aimlessly around his local shopping centre. The weather was very hot, especially for an August in Alefordshire, and so he decided to spend the week lazing in the garden reading. He decided to pop into his local bookshop.

But it seemed he was unable to get away from the case, as the first thing he saw was the promotion for "a stunningly good first work by a promising newcomer to the world of detective fiction" (Daily Moon). He recognised the author's name.

There was a short biography inside the rear cover. It read "The author, who writes under a pseudonym, is an expert on all aspects of criminal investigation. He is a renowned and experienced pathologist currently employed in Yorkshire, and has over twenty years' experience of working with the police in all matters medical."

He duly purchased "Pieces of a Jigsaw" by Robert Harrells.

It was good, he conceded, although he confessed he had rather hoped it wouldn't be … but he wasn't quite sure why. There were nineteen short stories, all well-written and cleverly-plotted, and all with a solid technical background. D.I. Pratt couldn't fault the author in terms of his knowledge of police procedures.

None of the stories bore any close resemblance to his recent enquiries, but he still had a niggling worry. Based on the state of the case as it stood at present, he thought his boss would hardly be likely to authorise him to visit Yorkshire to interview Robert Smith (for that was Robert Harrells' real name that he had noted from the file that Harry Black had shown him). But he was still on leave, with little to do, so he decided to visit his sister in Yorkshire.

Robert Smith lived in a small country cottage in the open countryside near Scarborough. He had said over the telephone that he would be in for D.I. Pratt to visit at an agreed time. D.I. Pratt had explained he was visiting his sister nearby, although he had neglected to say where, as Sheffield was rather more than a few minutes' drive away.

The cottage was obviously very old, and, equally obviously, very well restored and modernised. Each room was full of antiques and was decorated sympathetically. Any modern appliances such as a television or a computer were well hidden.

Having seen D.I. Pratt's credentials, and indeed having looked at them rigorously, Robert Smith smiled and relaxed in a large, comfortable chair, "So, is this an official enquiry?"

D.I. Pratt nodded vaguely, "It's a case - possibly murder - that I'm working on, and, as I'm on leave and staying nearby, I thought I could meet you and kill two birds with one stone." He stopped for a few seconds to consider if his choice of words could be construed as unfortunate, but there was only one woman involved, and so he continued.

"I was wondering about your book. Someone involved in the case seems to have read it, and we were wondering whether there was any link. I've just read "Pieces of a Jigsaw" myself, actually. Speaking as a member of the police force, I thought it was very well written, and I was wondering how you had gone about getting it published."

Robert Smith wondered if his advice were being sought so that D.I. Pratt could get his own work published, but continued nevertheless, "Well, the first literary agency I contacted was Sheila Wilson-Black, and they accepted me immediately. I don't think it's always that easy, especially as people only seem to want detective novels nowadays. Trying to publish a small book of twenty short detective stories isn't so easy these days, or so I would have thought, but Mr. Martin was very appreciative and supportive right from the start. He gave me a number of pieces of advice, constructive criticism I suppose you'd call it, and I naturally took his advice, but the finished article is almost exactly what I originally submitted. Martin seemed to like my style, and, of course, the technical details are all correct. The only real changes to the stories in the book were in the chapter I set in Victorian times. I'm afraid my historical research wasn't as good as my knowledge of current police procedures."

"So there were no major changes to the stories in the book, and you haven't submitted any other books to Wilson-Black's?" asked Pratt.

"The second book is almost ready for me to submit to Mr. Martin. It's not quite ready yet, so no-one has seen it."

Pratt sat back and mused for a few seconds. There didn't seem anything else he could think to ask. But there was something that troubled him at the back of his mind, even if he couldn't quite put it into words.

However, despite his anxiety, he started to relax a little more. Robert Smith seemed exceptionally good company, and an able raconteur. The conversation now became more social and less official. Smith told him of the time he was performing an autopsy when the "dead" body sat up and asked what he thought he was doing, although Pratt thought he had heard that somewhere else, and felt it may have been apocryphal. He returned with a story about when he had had to commandeer a hearse when his police car broke down during a high-speed car chase … although he'd actually seen that in a film.

In this way, a relaxed hour was spent exchanging pleasantries, although quite a few of these were not perhaps best described as pleasant.

D.I. Pratt looked at his watch. It was five o'clock, and time he returned.

He thanked Smith cordially for his help. Smith replied that things were often a little quiet up in the Scarborough area, and he was glad of the company.

It was only as Pratt had his hand on the garden gate that it came to him suddenly.

"There were twenty stories?" he asked.

"Mmm," replied Robert Smith, "Martin asked me to remove one of the stories, as he thought it too, er, "sensitive," I think he called it."

He found himself forced to welcome D.I. Pratt back into his lounge. Up until now, he had thought him pleasant enough company, although a bit sluggish and lacking in vitality, but now he revised his opinion. D.I. Pratt was like a youngster, full of energy and questions.

Robert Smith continued, "There again, I suppose it wasn't entirely Martin's idea. I first asked him whether he thought what was probably my best story should be included. The problem is that I know the business from the police side of things rather too well. I knew that a murder such as the one I described would go undetected by almost any medical officer even in an autopsy. So I asked Martin if I should drop it. He read it, and agreed most definitely. So I removed it, and, as there wasn't time to write another story, that left only nineteen stories."

"And what was this story about?"

D.I. Pratt hoped he already knew.

"Well, it was a case of poisoning. The poison was certainly not undetectable, but I knew that it wouldn't be traced by any standard medical tests. I suppose it might be if the case concerned the death of someone very important, royalty perhaps, or if the death were highly suspicious, but certainly not under normal circumstances."

"I think I'd better have a copy of the story, Robert," said D.I. Pratt. "The boys in the lab. might like to see it."

"And that's how I solved probably my greatest and most baffling case," said D.I. Pratt pompously. as he lay back in the uncomfortable armchair they had in his local pub.

"And so how *did* Martin kill his wife?" said Arnold Fisher, one of his oldest friends, who for once had not been bored by Pratt's tales of the local police force.

"Is it my round?" asked D.I. Pratt uncharacteristically.

Beyond a Joke

A diversion

"So, when this guy's wife asked how he knew she was having an affair, he told her it was because, whenever he left the house for work in the morning, he always made sure the toilet seat was down, and, on Wednesdays when he returned, it was always up!"

All Henry Dawkins' friends burst into spontaneous laughter at the end of George's joke. George always was the life and soul of the party, especially at the Golf Club.

In fact, Henry was the only one who wasn't laughing.

For Henry suddenly remembered that he had found his own toilet seat was up when he got home every Tuesday and Friday.

He resolved to monitor things a little more closely.

His wife became very impressed that he had finally started heeding her request for him to leave the toilet seat down. She actually said to all her friends that he'd be the most perfect man on earth if only he'd stop eating all those vile curries and that Mexican food.

But still, every Tuesday and Friday, the seat was always up when he got home.

In addition, he once found the end of a sizeable cigar partly-hidden under a soap dish in the bathroom. His wife didn't smoke, and he only enjoyed an occasional cigarette himself. Every week after that, he could always find at least a small piece of cigar leaf in the bathroom.

Henry didn't fancy a divorce, and so he discreetly checked with a few friends at the Golf Club as to how to hire someone to "remove a business rival who was making his life difficult."

Henry was flying to Glasgow on business on Monday and not returning for four nights. He made the necessary arrangements with the person he had hired, and, to be safe, only finalised things when he had actually checked in at his hotel in Glasgow. Henry was a cautious man, and didn't want to find his flight cancelled and his wife murdered just as he drove into their cul-de-sac.

But, settled into his comfortable suite at the Glasgow Hafton, he relaxed, sure in the knowledge that his problems would soon be over.

It was late afternoon on Tuesday when the person he had hired, Allan De'ath (yes, it was a pseudonym) parked a few blocks away from Henry's house and sauntered up to the address he had been given. There were no cars outside and no sounds inside, except for the gentle drone of a vacuum-cleaner.

He rang the doorbell and then had to wait whilst, he assumed, Mrs. Dawkins took off her apron, and tidied up her hair a little before opening the door.

Alicia Dawkins was a short petite blonde woman, the sort who might have been pretty enough to attract the eye of the boss when in her twenties, but who now only felt the need to enjoy the fruits of her labours, and had let herself become dowdy.

In death she looked even dowdier.

Her final dying thoughts were that she had thankfully finished cleaning the bathroom toilet, as she had done religiously every Tuesday and Friday for the last year, despite the deep revulsion she felt at the task. She had even had to smoke a vile cigar to mask the disgusting smells coming from the toilet after her husband's curries and Mexican meals.

Chapter 11

Through a Glass, Lightly

Cissy Raybould had no financial need to take in a lodger, or, as she phrased it, "a companion," but, for peace of mind, she felt safer with someone else in her large rambling house on the outskirts of Barrington, despite her only being in her early thirties.

So she put an advertisement in the local convenience shop window, advertising a room at what she hoped was an attractive rate. She wanted to keep it low so that she could choose the most suitable companion from a wide choice of applicants, rather than have only one or two to consider.

In fact, she was flooded with applicants, but had almost given up any hope of finding anybody even remotely suitable when Karen Banks arrived on her doorstep.

And they got on very well.

Karen was short, slim, blonde, and twenty-four years of age. She said she was pleasantly surprised that the rent was so low, as she had just started her own business, and she thought she wouldn't be able to afford "anything nice" until business picked up and she could increase her charges. She used some complicated name for her job, but, basically, she was an up-market shopfitter, specialising in refurbishing and updating offices.

And Karen's lifestyle suited Cissy very well. As Karen had little money at that stage of her career and needed to do a lot of planning and other paperwork, she hardly ever went out in the evenings. She had only recently moved south from her native York, where her friends and family lived, although, since her parents had died in a car crash when she was fifteen, there was really only her sister Mary, to whom she was very close.

So, Cissy was pleased that Karen was usually to be found in the house each evening, "just in case something happened."

As Cissy explained, she had a very weak heart, and had almost died once. She liked people to check fairly frequently that she was all right, up until the time she retired to bed, which was invariably very early.

So it was just as well that Karen was around when the local newspaper started carrying disturbing reports about a strange female figure seen in the neighbourhood. Tall, gaunt and pale, she always wore a dark suit, and appeared when and where she was least expected.

The local newspaper, 'The Alefordshire Gazette,' dubbed her 'The Barrington Vampire.'

Apart from frightening the very young and the elderly, the stories also sold a lot of extra newspapers.

Many folk decided to stay indoors after six o'clock, although the 'Vampire' invariably only appeared late at night or in the early hours of the morning. She never seemed to do very much, although one farmer maintained she was the reason some of his sheep had become ill after "blood had been taken."

After a while, everyone became accustomed to the stories, and, as nothing really sensational had happened, people started returning to their normal way of life and going out in the evenings again. The 'Vampire' did appear once or twice, but people just laughed at her now. The newspaper stopped running the stories. Its circulation didn't diminish though, as the Editor had realised where the money lay, and had already started up a new series of stories about a highly-unsubstantiated ghost seen near where a suicide had ended his life near Barrington Station.

"So what exactly do you do, Karen?" asked Cissy. "You seem to be working on something fairly important at the moment."

"Coleman Towers. An insurance company from America is taking over the second floor, so I have to arrange for all the computer wiring and electrics to be installed, refurbish the washrooms, and set up all the furniture, dividing it all into neat little cubicles. I've subcontracted a lot of the work, but it's still a lot for me to do. Still, the money's beginning to improve as I become better-known."

"I can increase your rent then," smiled Cissy, but Karen knew she was only joking.

"There's nobody in the office at the moment, as it's almost ready and the most of the subcontractors have finished. Call in and have a look at my handiwork tomorrow, if you like. Just ask for me at reception, and they'll call me down to collect you."

And so, at 1.30 p.m. as arranged, Cissy Raybould arrived at the reception desk at Coleman Towers.

At 2.30 p.m. she was dead.

Detective Chief Inspector Norman Muir liked his cases to be neat and simple. This certainly looked as if it were going to be.

"So?" he enquired vaguely.

He, his subordinate D.I. John Pratt, and Karen were sitting on some chairs in the corridor leading from the lifts to the main office on the second floor of Coleman Towers. They had avoided the chair on which Cissy Raybould had died. All the necessary tests having been done, Cissy's body had now been removed.

"Well," said Karen, "I rent a room from Miss Raybould, and, as she'd enquired about what exactly I did in my job, I invited her down here today. Oh God, I wish I hadn't."

"Do go on," muttered Muir unsympathetically.

"Well, she looked around the main room in there. She seemed interested in the cubicle system. I suppose she'd never seen that sort of thing before. I don't think she'd ever had a job."

"Anyway, we were just about to leave, when she said she wanted to visit the washroom. I assumed she wanted to go to the toilet, although, in retrospect, she might only have wanted to look at my work."

"So, she went in, and then she turned a very strange colour and staggered back. I helped her to the chair, and she collapsed into it, and, well, that was that. I got Dave on the reception desk to phone for an ambulance straight away."

Muir nodded and continued, "OK, this all seems very simple. You say she had a weak heart. If the autopsy findings agree with that as the cause of death, I'm sure we can close the case. So you can go home, Karen, when you're ready."

Pratt butted in, "We may need to look around a bit more before we all leave, Sir."

Muir was clearly a little upset at not being able to leave early. "And why might that be, Pratt?"

"Er, Miss Banks, which washroom did Miss Raybould go into?" Pratt asked.

"The one nearest the chair she was in. That door opposite. It's the ladies. The one next door to it is the gents. They're the last part of the refurbishment left to do. I was let down by the plumbers, and another firm is completing the job from tomorrow. I should still be on schedule though, I reckon."

Pratt asked, "Can we just have a look at the washroom, please?" He noticed he seemed to have upset Muir, who was beginning to fidget as the afternoon wore on.

"Certainly," said Karen, who got up and opened the door to the ladies washroom.

The ladies washroom seemed innocuous enough. Most things seemed to be working, including the flush toilets, but the taps weren't connected, and there was a large sheet of cardboard up on the wall where normally a large mirror would be fitted. Pratt lifted a corner of the cardboard to see if it were protecting a mirror underneath, but there was just a large hole there. He could see into the gents washroom on the other side.

Karen looked embarrassed. She clearly felt there was need for an explanation.

"Look, I'm not exactly sure if this is normal policy for American companies, but they said they wanted a large gap in the wall between the mirrors in the two washrooms. The possibility of installing some sort of surveillance device, such as a camera, was hinted at, but that wasn't my responsibility thankfully. Whatever they were going to do, it didn't sound very ethical."

Karen almost blushed, "Anyway, I certainly didn't install anything for them. I don't think I would have let myself be involved in something like that anyway, but thank God I wasn't asked to."

Pratt smiled. "Don't worry about that. I think we might ask somebody in a particular department to take a look at that when the office is up and running."

Karen brightened, "Well, if that's all, I'll be off home then. If you want me tonight, I'll be in the Travelodge in Darktown. I couldn't face Miss Raybould's house on my own tonight."

And she walked off towards the lifts.

Muir turned to Pratt. "I can't see anything of any interest here at all. Why did you decide that we needed to stay on for a little while?"

Pratt explained, "I just wanted to look around and see if there's anything in the washroom that might have upset Miss Raybould enough to trigger a heart attack."

He checked the gents washroom also. It looked exactly the same, but mirror-image. It also lacked taps and the mirror.

"OK," said Pratt, "I suppose you can go off and play golf now."

But Muir was already waiting for the lift.

The next day, Detective Chief Inspector Muir tossed a sheaf of papers onto the desk in front of John Pratt.

"Autopsy report. Heart attack. Her doctor confirms it could have happened at any time. Case closed. Golf this afternoon."

But, whilst Muir was playing golf, Pratt had a few enquiries of his own to make.

The next morning, Pratt was in Muir's room. He was in a talkative mood.

"Look, Sir, I had a few ideas when I saw the layout of the office, and I've checked up on a few things, and they all fit together."

Muir nodded sleepily, but was clearly quite happy to let Pratt talk on, especially if it meant he didn't have to do anything strenuous, such as think.

"OK, Sir, firstly, a few facts that I wondered about and which I've now checked."

Muir nodded again.

"Firstly, Cissy had no family, and her only beneficiary was Karen."

"That seemed likely anyway," muttered Muir.

"Secondly, Cissy was worried about that so-called vampire. She met the paper-boy on a number of occasions, after clearly lying in wait for him, to press him for any recent news."

"Hmm," said Muir.

"Thirdly, Karen's sister wasn't in York on the fateful afternoon. She was also staying in the Travelodge in Darktown."

Muir nodded, "Now, that is a bit more interesting. But it doesn't alter the facts about the heart attack, does it? It's still 'case closed.'"

Pratt shook his head. "I'm not so sure, but I don't know if there's anything we can do about it. Anyway, I'm pretty sure I know what happened."

Muir smiled patiently. "OK, go on then."

"Right, I think that Karen had been planning this in a vague sense for a while, but, when Cissy expressed an interest in seeing her work in this office, everything fell into place for her."

"She'd been enjoying herself worrying Cissy that she might be 'The Barrington Vampire.' She might have suggested she'd been sleepwalking perhaps, and it looks as if Cissy was quite worked up about it."

"When Cissy called into Coleman Towers, she might have asked to see the washroom, or perhaps it was suggested she should. Karen would have gone in first, perhaps saying she had to check that the workmen had left it safe, and then Cissy would have walked in … to see Karen reflected in the mirror …"

"… But not herself."

"She'd see she had no reflection!"

"Coming on top of her worries about being the vampire, that shock might just have finished her off. She was helped onto the chair in the corridor, where she passed away."

"Well," said Muir, "Most of it sounds good, even quite likely, but you can't explain why she mightn't have had a reflection. *Was* she a vampire?"

Pratt smiled. "Karen had merely taken down the cardboard, so that the one washroom looked into the other, which was an exact copy, but mirror-image. Her sister, made-up to look like her, and wearing similar clothes, was mirroring her actions in the other room. The gents washroom, that is."

"Cissy thought it was a mirror, and that Karen's sister was Karen's reflection, but the mirror was really just a rectangular gap in the wall where you'd expect a mirror to be."

"I'm impressed," said Muir, "But can we prove all that?"

Pratt continued, "I reckon the only way you'd prove it is if one of the sisters confessed. I can hardly see that happening."

"And, even if we could prove it, what could we do? We would have a very slim chance of proving even manslaughter."

Pratt had a long think, and came to a decision.

He went with Muir for a round of golf.

Chapter 12

Dead and Breakfast

I wouldn't say I am normally an impulsive buyer, but, when I was holidaying in Tenby to celebrate my Uncle Gerry passing away and leaving me his inheritance, and I saw this darling little boutique hotel up for sale, and, for the first time in my life, I could afford it ... well, even without any experience in the business whatsoever, wouldn't you have bought it?

But I certainly hadn't been making much money out of it. August's bookings had been acceptable, but, even with Christmas fast approaching, my bookings were all but non-existent.

And then I had a brainwave. I would hold a Murder Mystery Weekend at the hotel in the days just prior to Christmas. I could increase my prices to more than cover the additional costs, and make a real profit for once.

So, to gain some experience, I booked myself onto a similar weekend at an established chain of hotels (I must say I was very impressed with the way the hotel was run ... far better than mine is). And I made notes, so that, even though I was the only one not to realise that the murderer was the deranged wife of the butler, I felt sure I had taken enough details to be able to stage such a weekend ourselves.

My chef, well I suppose 'cook' is a more appropriate term, and I worked out a rather impressive meal, with a lot of fancy, expensive food that we would never normally have bought, and we had one of the local teachers translate it into French for us. I managed to rope in a lot of my friends who were willing to perform just for the fun of it. And I even spent a fair bit of money on publicising the weekend ... and the hotel was full within hours!

I just had to make sure this was a resounding success for us to be able to stage it regularly. And then I could become every so slightly rich!

I don't want to give away anything of the plot, but two of my friends were going to be elderly spinsters supposedly staying at the hotel, and I had three other friends playing extra members of staff. Cook and I would be more or less playing ourselves within the mystery too.

I had worked really hard at this project of mine, going over everything very carefully, so that nothing could go wrong. The food had been ordered weeks beforehand from a dependable supplier. I had extra (non-acting) staff available in the town if necessary. And I had all the weapons and props needed for the mystery, including a few red herrings.

My only fear was that some of the guests wouldn't turn up, and my profits would plummet.

But I needn't have worried. All my guests arrived punctually on the Friday, some even a little early. I'd specified that the weekend would start after 3.00 p.m., and it was quite a surprise to find all twenty-four guests huddling in our reception area at the third stroke of my grandfather clock.

Now nothing could go wrong! Short of a real murder, that is.

But, as usual, I was wrong.

When the guests had gone up to their rooms, Cook appeared, twisting her apron and looking dejected.

"Bellman's have rung," she said quietly. "They can't deliver until early tomorrow morning, And I've tried everywhere to find alternative sources. Nobody around here stocks the sort of food we've ordered."

I would have loved to have reassured her and told her not to worry, but all the guests had received the menus, and they would be expecting the meals to bear at least some slight resemblance to those specified.

The plan had been to let everyone settle in and get the feel of the hotel, before assembling in the lounge and meeting some of the possible victims and perpetrators. Then the murder!

Julie Robinson, my friend who runs the local newsagent's, was usually busy, but she had said she would be able to turn up around tea-time on Friday, as long as she wouldn't be needed after seven. Well, she'd be long dead by then, so that was no problem.

Whilst we left the "Police" to investigate and look for fingerprints, we'd all have our dinner. The guests would have plenty of time to discuss what had happened and compare notes afterwards.

I was particularly proud of the menu Cook and I had drawn up. It started with "Filet de saumon, pomme et jus de verveine," followed by ... but all that's irrelevant now.

"Hang on," said Cook (her surname really was Cook), "Are you sure we can't just hope none of them can understand a word of French, and give them something from the bowels of our freezer?"

"Yes!" I squealed, and then, deflated, added, "No, you forget that we have a Madame Dubois down from London. She'll know!"

And then I had a brainwave, the second this year!

I had a word with Cook, and then phoned Julie and said she wouldn't be needed.

Then I called all the guests into the reception area, where they were clearly expecting someone to be murdered.

Suddenly there was a scream from the kitchen!

We all rushed in, to find Cook lying on the preparation table (most unhygienic!) with a huge and rather unlikely African knife sticking out of her stomach.

"Aargh! Aargh! It was … it was ... it was that ..." she said unconvincingly, although no less unconvincingly than in many television programmes. She slumped to one side.

I held everybody back and announced, "I suggest we withdraw to the dining-room until the Police have arrived and completed their investigations. Then they'll make a report to us, and there'll be plenty of time for you all to investigate and deliberate afterwards."

I took a deep breath and then looked resigned. With a slight shrug, I added "I am afraid that, with poor Cook lying here brutally slain, we shall have to have sandwiches tonight."

And everyone, thankfully, nodded sagely.

Maybe buying the Hotel *had* been a good idea after all!

Chapter 13

The Wrong Man

John Pratt turned his four-year-old Ford Focus off the hot tarmac of the Route Nationale onto a smaller side road, and, for the first time since arriving in France, felt some small degree of confidence that he was on the right road at last. Not only could he see the first clear road-sign for his destination of Segnolles, but he could also see what he felt sure was the small town on a little hill in the distance.

He drove steadily along the road, pleased to be away from the mad rush of French traffic, half of it seeming to consist of farmers in battered old Peugeots with only two gears, the other half of BMW drivers late for an appointment. This road suited him though. On either side were serried ranks of vines, and the pleasant, though unidentified, smell of the countryside complemented the insistent drone of the cicadas. He wondered how anything that small could make such a racket.

This was one of John's rare trips abroad. As a detective inspector, he usually felt that he was unable to take much time away from his work, but a long-running disagreement with a senior colleague had forced him to re-evaluate his need for a rest, and so he had visited his local travel agency. Eschewing the many package holidays offered, he had insisted on having the ferry and the hotel accommodation booked individually for him in the area of France he had decided upon, and this had greatly taxed the travel agent's ability, so that making the reservations had taken far longer than John would have expected.

Segnolles was an ancient bastide town, encircled by the almost-compete remains of the town wall, and with the streets all laid out in a perpendicular grid system, something that John had assumed was very much a twentieth-century idea. Having found Segnolles, he now had to find his accommodation. He did try asking the local inhabitants for directions, but he found their replies rather confusing and even contradictory. In the end, he decided to put his faith in some higher agency, and so, ignoring all instructions and signs, he drove straight to where he felt the hotel should be ... and found it almost immediately.

As he had expected the photographs of the hotel to be fancifully inaccurate, he was pleasantly surprised (but only just) when he actually saw the establishment. It was just off the main square (although the approach by car was exceedingly complex and tortuous), and looked just the same as the private houses on either side (the photographs had presumably been taken from the garden, as it had appeared that the hotel was standing in its own grounds). Car parking facilities, it was announced, were in the main square, but John saw no reason why he shouldn't just park outside, and so he did so, squeezing the Focus in between two large delivery vans. A decidedly mangy-looking cat watched him park from the top of a wall, before scratching itself, and then hopping through a first-floor window into the hotel. John hoped that that wasn't his bedroom.

The foyer of the hotel was surprisingly cool, considering the heat outside. Also surprising was that there was a receptionist of sorts. Normally, in anything other than a major hotel, one has to shout towards the kitchens before anyone official can be found.

John hadn't realised quite how British he looked, but the man at the reception desk (a nameplate proclaimed him to be a Monsieur Papin) enquired in English, "Can I help?" Sounding the aitch in 'help' seemed to cause him quite an effort.

"John Pratt," John announced.

M. Papin checked the register and handed him the key to his room. It was marked "302."

John was a little taken aback, as he didn't think that the hotel looked as if it had more than twenty rooms at the most. He wondered if the hotel had bought a job lot of assorted hotel key fobs, and had then assigned the room numbers accordingly.

"Don't you want me to register?" he asked.

M. Papin shook his head. "The Saturday staff booked you in yesterday. You don't need to register again."

John didn't really understand what he was being told about "booking in yesterday," but he was tired, and just wanted to lie down in his own room for a while before "hitting the town" (John smiled as he thought of this phrase).

His room was small, cool, fairly clean, and cat-less, with a small window overlooking the street in front.

It was also occupied.

The bed had been made (this was now around four on the Sunday afternoon), but there was a small overnight bag beside the door, various toiletries in the bathroom, and a few clothes and other things in the wardrobe.

John wandered back down to the reception area. M. Papin was still there.

"Have I got the wrong room?" John asked. "There's a bag, some clothes, and toothbrushes and things in the bathroom."

M. Papin frowned, "Are they not your things? Didn't you take them up when you arrived yesterday?"

"I've only just arrived," John spluttered. "I stopped last night in a little plastic box of a room in a hotel on an industrial estate outside Paris."

M. Papin thought deeply. "Then they're not your things?"

As he seemed unable to think of anything else to say, John decided to take the initiative, and, leaning across the counter, spun the registrar around so that he could read it. Sure enough, against the previous day's entries for Saturday was written "John Pratt," with the address simply "U.K."

John really didn't know what was going on. "Look," he said, "If my doppelganger should return, please call me to come down and meet him. And the same applies to the member of staff who checked him in yesterday. In the meantime, I shall leave all the clothes and things in my room locked in the, er, *my* wardrobe. O.K.?"

M. Papin suddenly remembered something. "Oh, there's a note to say that you told the receptionist yesterday that you'd show your passport today."

John handed it over.

M. Papin beamed. "There," he said, "So you *are* M. Pratt after all, eh?"

The reason why John had decided on this particular holiday was that he wanted to paint. He had read that some of the more famous impressionists had painted in the area, and hoped he might derive some inspiration from the same locations and atmosphere, not that he was very accomplished, as he would be the first to admit.

So, after a fairly undisturbed sleep and an insufficiently-disturbed breakfast, he took his easel and various boxes with him, and wandered off to find somewhere peaceful and inspiring.

The weather was warm but very overcast, with dark rain-clouds always threatening. Although there were vines rather than wheat, a few crows in the near distance put John in mind of some of Van Gogh's paintings, and so he decided to set up his easel very close to the vineyards on the south side of the town.

John was not one of these pretentious painters who "must have the muse with them." But, even though he wasn't really very good, he did need to be able to immerse himself completely in his attempts.

And that was one thing he could not do. Try as he might, he could not get his room's other occupant out of his mind. For most of the time, instead of applying paint to canvas, he found himself trying to fathom out what could have happened.

How would anyone know that John would be staying there that week, and from where did they get his name? He supposed that perhaps a friend of a member of the hotel staff might have decided to book in for the night, hoping that John wouldn't notice when he paid the bill on Friday, but why should he leave all his clothes there? If he had been unable to return for them for some reason, surely his friend in the hotel could have collected them for him? Anyway, John had tried on some of the clothes for size, and they fitted him well enough, so he decided that, if prompted, he would pay for the additional night he had not taken, and keep the clothes for himself - after all, they were supposed to be his, weren't they? They seemed quite trendy anyway. John had nothing like that in his wardrobe at home.

But could there be some deeper motive? He was struggling to remember some Hitchcock film he had seen on television recently, something that seemed similar to his predicament.

'North by Northwest,' that was it! He remembered the plot, or some of it, a little better than the cast, but was sure James Stewart and Grace Kelly were in it.

The character played by James Stewart - or was it Cary Grant? - found his life converging with that of a Mr. Kaplan, a non-existent secret agent invented by the CIA to draw attention away from the real agent, who was close to the arch-villain. The villain wanted Kaplan dead, so the character played by, yes, he was sure it was Cary Grant spent the whole of the film trying to convince both sides who he really was. Was the film really that simple? He seemed to remember he got lost trying to follow it at the time.

But, no, that could hardly explain this situation. There was no non-existent character for him to be mistaken for. In this situation, there was only one person ... but two people claiming to be that person!

He decided to try to return to his original resolution of ignoring the problem and concentrating on his painting.

It was on Wednesday that he finally accepted that that wasn't going to be possible. He had been so preoccupied with thinking about the second Mr. Pratt that he had only managed to paint a few vague shapes, and, after a few minutes, he found that he just could not remember what they were meant to be.

Apart from trying to think out the puzzle himself, he had made a few enquiries, not that there were many avenues open to him that he could think of. The Saturday receptionist was apparently away with his family for a week in the next region, and no-one had been to claim the clothes. With regard to his ideas about the Hitchcock film, there appeared to be a marked lack of espionage in the sleepy little town.

But now it was Wednesday, and John had only two more nights in the hotel. He felt he had to try something, if only for his own peace of mind.

He called into the local police station to speak with the gendarmerie.

Unfortunately, the local police didn't have anyone available who spoke English (they were probably worried about the legal implications of saying the wrong thing in a foreign language, he thought), and so John was forced to fall back on his schoolboy French, desperately trying to remember to avoid words such as 'flic' and 'poulet,' and trying not to say 'tu' to a policeman unless he wanted several nights in gaol (or so Monsieur Braithwaite, his old French master had said).

Despite the relatively small content of the conversation between John and the gendarme on the desk, it was a measure of John's ability to converse in French that this short exchange of words took almost twenty minutes.

A (much) condensed and translated version follows.

"Is there anyone English staying in Segnolles at the moment?" John asked.

The gendarme's face brightened, "Yes, yes, there is an Englishman staying at the Hotel de Segnolles." That was John's hotel. It was also clearly John to whom he referred.

He tried another approach, "Has anything unusual or strange happened here in town recently, say, since last Saturday?"

"In Segnolles? But it's always so peaceful and tranquil here. If you want excitement, try Tremont."

Tremont was apparently viewed by the locals as a hotbed of all that was sinful and worthwhile in life, or so it may have seemed to the locals. In fact, John guessed, correctly as it turned out, that it was merely the nearest large town, and as such a rival, but in fact no more lascivious or less God-fearing than anywhere else.

It was only a few kilometres away, so John resolved to visit it that morning. It was in fact slightly more than the few kilometres that John had thought, as he hadn't realised that the gendarme had converted the distance into miles for him, but it was a pleasant enough drive through the morning sun, amidst the vines and the few shady trees.

Tremont was almost everything Segnolles was not. It was ugly, large, sprawling, certainly not picturesque, and dedicated to industry and commerce. However, the promised Sodom, rife with all forms of crime, gambling and sexual deviancy, did not seem evident, and

John thought it unlikely he would find the answer to his enigma here. He drove around for a while, seeing nothing of interest, and then arrived at one of the large commercial complexes that the French seem to love so much. He decided he ought to stock up on wine and whisky for the return journey, and parked in the car park of a hypermarket there.

As usual, all the French seemed to have tried to park as close to the entrance of the store as possible, but John decided that, even though his car was four years old, he would prefer to park it farther away in an area where there were less likely to be other cars parking alongside. That way, he hoped he wouldn't return to find someone had opened their car door and dented one of his. There was a nice shaded area on the other side of the car park, so he made for that.

And there, parked under the trees, was a small red Vauxhall from his own part of Britain. Another Englishman had obviously been of the same mind as he, but where was the owner? The driver's door was very badly dented, obviously from some traffic accident, and one of the tyres was flat. It looked as if the car had been there for quite a few days.

John thought, "Since Saturday or Sunday?"

Things began to get a little clearer in his mind.

Forgetting his intended purchases, he drove out of the car park. The squeal of tyres was uncharacteristic of him.

Although his next visit was originally to have been the police station in Tremont, he now drove to the local hospital. He had seen some signs for it whilst driving through the outskirts of the town, and so he now headed in that direction. The signs were, for once, quite accurate, and the girl in the hospital reception area spoke English well, and so he was outside James Wells' room within a quarter-of-an-hour.

He didn't know the name, and, on entering the room, found the occupant asleep, but he immediately recognised the travel agent who had had so much trouble making the travel reservations for him back in England.

His attempt to spend an extra night in a hotel on the way to his own holiday destination without paying might have worked if his car hadn't been hit by another car in the hypermarket car park whilst he was shopping on the Sunday morning.

Chapter 14

You Hang Around Waiting for Hours ...

Margaret Cox spoke in a well-modulated, controlled voice, but D.I. John Pratt reckoned he had about five minutes with her before she broke down in tears.

"Well usually, Candy ... her real name's Belinda ..." Margaret Cox hesitated for a few seconds.

"But she was as sweet as candy?" prompted Pratt.

"No, she was always eating sweets and chocolates. Come to think of it, she was rather overweight ... and her teeth were pretty awful."

"Anyway, after bingo, we usually walked with each other part of the way home. But last night it looked like rain, so she only went with me as far as the nearest bus stop. We got there at exactly eight o'clock by the church clock just over the road."

Pratt nodded. He'd already checked the accuracy of the clock, after Margaret had made an initial short statement to a colleague.

"It was only two stops from there for her, just to the terminus at Rotham. I was going to wait with her until the bus arrived, but, as Candy pointed out, it was only about five minutes to wait, and the clouds did look threatening. Anyway, there's no bus route to my house, so I set off on my own. Now, I'll never see her again."

Margaret Cox went off to sit down in a corner. Pratt decided his five minutes were nearly up.

Candy Fennell had been found early that morning on the moors on the other side of Battersby. She had been raped and strangled.

But Candy had been seen by quite a few people whilst she had waited for her bus.

Opposite the bus stop, there was a small taxi office. The receptionist there, a Miss Jean Hole, had looked out of the window quite frequently, as there was a fare waiting for Harry, and he was running late as his sat nav was on the blink. She could confirm that she had seen Candy waiting for about five minutes, but had not seen anybody else waiting at the stop or talking to Candy, had not seen any vehicle other than the bus pull up, and, naturally, there had been no-one at the stop after the bus had left, almost immediately after which Harry turned up. She hadn't seen Candy walking away from the stop either.

This had been corroborated by the owner of the small café by the bus stop, as well as by as many of those eating there as could be traced, mainly the regulars.

So, nobody had seen Candy leave the bus stop on foot, and nobody had seen any vehicle other than the bus pull up.

Pratt had interviewed Ted Burke, a bus driver working for the 'Portway Line,' at their depot. He said he had arrived on time at the bus stop, at 2008, and had stopped there even though there appeared to be no-one waiting or wanting to get off. As he said, sometimes someone makes a last minute dash, perhaps from the café, and anyway it wasn't a request stop. But no-one had got on or off. And there were plenty of passengers to confirm his story. Ted also confirmed that there weren't any other scheduled services using that road that Candy could have caught. That should have saved Pratt quite a bit of work, but he checked it himself anyway.

The fact that no-one had seen Candy either accept a lift or walk away from the stop didn't of course mean that she hadn't done either. However, with eight people watching, albeit intermittently, it seemed odd that no-one had seen anything of interest.

Anyway, Margaret Cox had already confirmed that she was certain that, under no circumstances, would Candy have accepted a lift from anyone she didn't know, and, with a very limited circle of friends that basically included just Margaret Cox, that reduced the list of suspects to professional acquaintances such as her doctor and her dentist.

However, upon investigation, no-one in this category could be considered a suspect.

Having checked with those watching and with the meteorologists, Pratt decided that it seemed unlikely that Candy would have left the shelter of the bus stop to walk home at that time, as it had already started to rain quite heavily. Despite being open on three sides, the shelter afforded some cover at least.

So, if she didn't get on Ted Burke's bus and didn't walk home through the rain, Candy must have accepted a lift – but who would be able to induce her to get into their vehicle so quickly, without argument, that no-one else noticed that vehicle?

After a few days, Pratt had really got nowhere with the case, except, as he thought to himself with some comfort, that he had been able to rule out several possible options.

Unfortunately, as he also thought to himself, he had been able to rule out *all* possible options.

Then he had a germ of an idea.

But how could he prove it?

Then he remembered a colleague in the force who might be able to help. He was a decent enough chap, and performed his job well, but ... well, his conversation was a little limited.

Charlie King was perfectly happy to help.

"Well, I think most people would be suspicious if something other than one of Portway's red-and-green double-deckers pulled up at the bus stop. So, if you think two buses may have stopped there that night, and you've checked that all Portway's are accounted for, I think we're looking for someone who owns a double-decker that looks at least a little like one of Portway's, perhaps some small private operator or a preservationist."

His face brightened.

"And who better than Dave Lee? He has an old preserved Portway Leyland! There was a rally down in Dorset last weekend, and he probably would have taken it there. And he might very well have passed that bus stop on his return, at the very time you're interested in. Personally, I've never liked Dave that much. He seems rather an odd sort."

Coming from Charlie King that was quite a condemnation, Pratt thought.

Dave Lee lived on his father's farm, towards Pentlesham.

His beloved double-decker was in his barn.

There was plenty of evidence on it.

Chapter 15

Requiem Symphony

It wasn't that Barry Williams was ungrateful. He had written more jingles for television commercials than anyone else in the business, and had become fairly rich as a result. But, somehow he couldn't see himself earning a place in history on that basis.

Barry hoped his new symphony would do that.

He knocked gently on his agent's door, and then ambled in.

"We haven't seen very much of you recently, Barry. Some of our clients have been getting a little upset having to use your colleagues instead of you, but they'll come back now you're available again."

"So, the symphony is finally finished, eh? It's taken you long enough, but then you always were a perfectionist." H. Parkinson Wentworth held out his hand.

Barry handed over the score. "It's written in a vaguely classical style and format, but using themes that are a little more up-to-date. It should appeal to anyone but a die-hard purist."

Wentworth nodded. "That sort of thing is fairly popular at the moment, but there aren't many who have either the ability or the time. Can I hear some of it?"

Barry set the score on the piano and played a few pages. He was surprised to see his agent looking at first a little upset, and finally almost apoplectic.

"Is this some kind of a joke, Barry?"

Barry assured him it wasn't. "I've worked night and day on this for months. It's my first major work, and I've used ideas and themes I've been developing since my university days. What's wrong?"

H. Parkinson Wentworth twiddled with a radio that was on the desk. He had to check only a few stations before he found what he was searching for - Barry's Symphony.

Barry left the office in a state of shock.

On the way home, he called into his local music store and bought a CD of Haydn Britain's 'Symphony for Today.' He played it as soon as he got home.

It wasn't as polished as Barry's work. It had quite a few rough edges, and the last movement was much shorter, without his final triumphant climax. Someone had clearly decided to rush through the final scoring, and get it recorded and in the shops well before Barry would have considered his work ready for an audience.

But it was still good.

Of course it was, thought Barry, it's mine!

Barry wondered who Haydn Britain was. The notes accompanying the CD gave little away. Haydn Britain was clearly a pseudonym for someone in the same industry as Barry.

But the question wasn't who, but how.

Many people knew that Barry had been writing a large-scale work for some time, but how could they copy his music?

He checked his house for any recording devices, not totally sure for what he was looking.

Then he remembered the telephone engineer who had arrived unannounced to check if he were "experiencing similar problems to others in the street." At the time, he had thought it strange that the engineer had only been interested in the extension in his music room, but that didn't seem to be a problem then.

Yes, he was certain that that must be where the bug had been hidden.

So, should he disconnect the phone ?

No.

Barry had murder in mind.

Even though he didn't know exactly who had engineered the theft, Barry had mentally drawn up a shortlist on which were the names of a number of young composers, each trying to make his mark in the music business, and each keen to achieve overnight the same status that Barry had worked for fifteen years to achieve.

He wasn't sure whether it was possible to trace who had placed the bug in his telephone, but he didn't really want to call in any experts, or involve anyone else. He had other plans.

Barry had never been one to relax and take a rest. So, he set to work immediately on another major work, a symphony that was a fusion of classical music and modern jazz. By this time, he had hoped to be writing his second symphony, but he was resigned to the next new symphony he wrote being his first now.

As with his ill-fated first major work, the themes had been flowing around in Barry's head for many years. Now he started working on them in more depth, trying them out on the piano and making a few notes until he felt he had something worthy of committing to paper properly. One would have thought that, after the manner of the theft of his first symphony, he would have finished this as quickly as possible, but no, perfectionist as he was, he worked on the themes for each of the five movements and developed them completely before returning to polish up the work as a whole.

In fact, work on this symphony seemed to be taking almost as long as on the first, as Barry decided that, having worked fruitlessly without income for so long on the first symphony, his finances dictated that he would have to accept other commissions at the same time.

Some major clients were pleased to find that he was quite willing to take on their more menial, but vastly more profitable, work whilst he was tidying up his symphony.

Indeed, for a considerable number of months, Barry had largely cut himself off from the outside world, not finalising the symphony, but writing a set of themes for a new espionage television series.

With these new scores in his briefcase, he returned to his agent's office.

H. Parkinson Wentworth was pleased. "Great! There'll probably be a couple of re-writes and re-workings knowing this mob, but not too many I would have thought. It's just what they want, I'm sure."

Barry turned to leave, and had the door half-open before his agent called him back.

"Did you hear about Haydn Britain?" he asked.

"No," replied Barry truthfully, although he had a fair idea what he was about to be told.

"He published his second major work two weeks ago. Most people thought it was a brilliant new five-movement jazz symphony."

"But the whole thing had been lifted from some film composer's jazz symphony of the sixties or seventies ... and almost note-for-note too! Anyway, someone tipped off the original composer's agent about what was happening. There's no way Haydn Britain's getting out of this. He's being taken to court next month."

"In fact, I think we've witnessed the death of Haydn Britain."

Barry tried to smile sympathetically.

In the Library with Theo Dagger

A diversion

You may not heave heard of Theo Dagger, but you will certainly have heard of Marie Franck, the plucky female French detective created by Dorothy Hilton.

Well, the character of Marie was actually based on Theo, and most of, and probably the best of, the stories about her were based on actual cases solved by Theo, who was originally a Detective Inspector in the CID, and latterly a private investigator. And, since retiring, he has become a much sought-after after-dinner speaker and raconteur, even if he is now well into his eighties..

So, as he is also a not-too-distant neighbour, when I decided to invite a few friends around for a soirée, I made the natural decision to invite him, even if that did make the number thirteen.

After an excellent dinner, we all repaired to the library, where I was hoping the ambience of the classic English detective story location would work wonders on Mr. Dagger's story-telling abilities and, probably, ego.

Everyone there knew of his prowess and deductive powers (in case it were otherwise, I had in fact told all my guests beforehand), so everyone gathered at his feet whilst he sat in my most comfortable winged armchair.

He clearly knew why he had been invited and did not disappoint.

"I remember one case," he said, his head wreathed in a dense pall of smoke from his pipe, "Which happened in a country house a little like this, but perhaps a few miles down the road."

Everyone was clearly thinking deeply, trying to work out which of the many such homes in the locality it might be.

"The elderly gentleman who owned the house, an eminent doctor of some standing in the county, had been murdered, and, as there were certain factors that were a little, shall we say, embarrassing, I was called in immediately, before the local police were informed."

"It was obvious from the start that nobody had left the premises as the doors were all locked from the inside. On closer inspection, nobody could have got in or out of the house without making it obvious. So, as all the staff had prepared for the evening and then been given the night off, the only suspects were the six guests who had been invited to the house that evening. They clearly wanted me to arrive at a solution quickly before the rather heavy-footed local constabulary was summoned."

"So, on the face of it, it was a fairly simple little mystery: one body, six suspects, no possibility of anybody else being involved. I set to work, using my usual techniques."

"I gathered the six suspects together in the library, and their stories all seemed to agree. They had finished dinner, and were relaxing over port and a few cigars in that very room, when they realised their host was absent. They all went off to search for him, but couldn't find him on the ground floor or the upper storey. Eventually, they found Dr. Black's body at the foot of the stairs leading to the cellar, where he had clearly been dragged after having been brutally murdered. But who had done this heinous deed?"

"I began at once a minute inspection of all the rooms. I was a little suspicious of the fact that the country house had been built during the period when many British Catholics were being persecuted. Were there perhaps priest holes or some other well-concealed hiding-places in the house … or secret passages by which a murderer might move from one location to another without being seen?"

"My first find was in the kitchen. It was cleverly concealed, but not cleverly enough to remain hidden from old Theo's prying eyes. There was a hidden catch, which revealed a secret passageway all the way to the other side of the house. I suspected there might be others. Now at last we were getting somewhere!"

"Next, I decided to talk to each suspect individually. I decided on the three women first. One was very young and attractive, attired in a rather raunchy red outfit. I spent some time interviewing her, and perhaps a little less time on the other two." Here, Theo gave a broad wink, which was more than a little unsettling.

"In fact, I discovered all three women were only distantly acquainted with the deceased. All had been rather surprised to be invited to such an apparently intimate evening, and could shed no further light on the events that day."

"Next, I decided to interview the three men. It had in fact been the Professor, the Colonel and the Reverend who had eventually found their host, or rather, ex-host, on venturing into the cellars, apparently looking for another bottle of a rather excellent Chateau Lafite."

For the first time, someone - myself - interrupted the raconteur.

"Speaking of which," I said, "If you'd excuse me, I rather think we could all do with some more wine ourselves." I went off to the cellar on my own.

For some reason, the bulb didn't work in the cellar. I didn't bother checking for the fuse, as I knew my way around pretty well.

It was while I was feeling for the banister on the stairs to make my way back that I realised I was not alone in the cellar. I heard scuffling behind me, and then an oath.

"Do you always buy the cheapest bulbs?" muttered Freddie Langley, one of my guests. I smiled.

"Sorry to frighten you," he said, "But I wondered why you left us. None of us had empty glasses, and I would have thought you in particular would have been enthralled with old Theo Dagger's story."

It was my turn to curse.

"He must have been a great man at one time, but he's clearly senile now."

"What do you mean?" countered Freddie, "It's a great story, and I'm only missing it because, after the way you left the group on such a clearly false errand, I was worried that you weren't feeling well."

"Great story? *Great story?*" I could hardly believe Freddie's stupidity.

"He's so senile, he's getting fact and fiction all mixed up. That's not a case he's worked on that he's telling you about, you know."

Freddie still looked blank.

"It's obviously just a Cluedo game he once played."

Freddie and I burst into laughter, so loudly that the rest of the guests left old Theo Dagger alone with his memories, and came to see what was happening.

Chapter 16

And Two Number 46 with Rice, Please

Arthur New and his wife were clearly in a distracted mood. They had covered their dining-room table with plates of cakes and biscuits, together with a little three-tiered porcelain cake-stand laden with slices of Battenberg cake, but had neglected to offer any of it to D.I. John Pratt. Arthur had even poured out the tea without bothering to offer milk, and, whilst there was a little cow-shaped milk jug on the table, it was empty. Mr. and Mrs. New certainly didn't look like the sort of people not to take milk with their tea, and D.I. Pratt wondered whether they just didn't realise what they were drinking.

"Look," Arthur whispered, "I know what you're probably thinking. I've read a lot of police novels myself. You're probably wondering whether my wife and I are lying to give Bob an alibi."

"Well I can assure you that Shirley and I don't think much of Bob, to put it mildly, and probably wouldn't put it past him to do something as terrible as this. So we'd never give that little ... er, an alibi unless we were absolutely certain. We adored our June, you know. She was everything a daughter should be."

D.I. Pratt had already decided that the couple were totally honest, but, yes, the thought had crossed his mind, and so it was nice to be reassured.

The preceding November evening, Bob, uncharacteristically, had arranged to collect his parents from the local railway station ("Dead on time, six thirty-one") and to cook a meal for them. Apparently, Arthur had once worked on the railways, and had a keen interest in their efficiency or otherwise ("It's not like God's Wonderful Railway these days, mind you"). So their son's offer for them to visit him for a meal and for him to pay for the train had seemed a bit of an adventure, even if neither of them really liked their son.

He had picked them up and taken them to a huge new Barris housing development in Rotham, a dormitory town some distance outside Aleford, where his three-bedroom detached house was. He had recently attended a Chinese cookery course at night school, and was keen to demonstrate his newly-acquired skills to his parents, who, although a little unsure about oriental cuisine, were willing "to give it a go," on condition Bob didn't make it too spicy.

The meal had gone uneventfully, and they had left at quarter to ten to get back to the station to catch the 22.14 ("Two whole minutes late," bemoaned Arthur).

D.I. Pratt had been most precise on the point of timing. "And are you absolutely positive that Bob never left you for more than two minutes?"

Both had been adamant. He had only left them for a maximum of two minutes every now and then to pop into the kitchen.

And June had been tied up and stabbed in her own garage at some time between seven-thirty and nine.

June New had lived as a single parent at 38 Aspen Avenue on the same housing development as her brother. Her house was almost totally devoid of clutter or ornamentation, but the reason was apparent when Pratt ventured upstairs: one bedroom was clearly hers, another was her daughter's, and the third was for everything that wouldn't fit neatly into a cupboard elsewhere.

Still there was little of interest here. Downstairs, the focus of attention had to be the garage, where June's body, still bound and gagged, had been found by her daughter, returning around eleven from a party.

According to both her mother and her daughter, June had had very few acquaintances at all, let alone enemies (this was later confirmed at the school where she worked). Her estranged husband lived in Australia, and had been confirmed as not having left since his arrival seven years previously.

There was little of further interest downstairs. The kitchen was clean, and it appeared that June had not eaten much, if anything at all, that evening. Certainly everything was spotless and there was only a slight smell of cooking. The lounge / dining-room was similarly tidy.

Yesterday must have been a busy day for her, as the morning post, unopened and probably delivered after she had left for work, together with an evening newspaper and a magazine, were still on the hall table.

D.I. Pratt looked through the post to see if it suggested any enemies, perhaps someone to whom she owed money. There was only a bill from Barclaycard, but they rarely took outstanding amounts that personally, thought Pratt.

The newspaper and magazine had presumably been delivered late afternoon or early evening by the local paper-boy. The magazine was 'Practical Electronics.'

There was no other indication in the house that June had had such an interest. D.I. Pratt phoned her parents. Arthur New answered.

"Electronics? She hated anything newfangled like that," was the reply.

Early in the afternoon, D.I. Pratt interviewed Bob New at his house on the other side of the estate. Even if it was on the same estate, it was still eight minutes' drive away because of all the cul-de-sacs and other devices incorporated to try and increase the number of houses per square mile. Walking would have taken even longer. He drove from streets named after trees, through areas where they were named after poets, London theatres, television comedians, battles, authors, and finally composers. He drove along Walton Way, Beethoven Boulevard, Chopin Crescent, Ravel Road, and finally Presley Parade. Bob lived at number 46, about half-way along.

There was very little he really wanted to ask. He had already obtained detailed timings from Bob's parents, and had established that Bob liked neither his parents nor his sister, although whether the enmity between Bob and June was sufficient to warrant murder he wasn't sure. Not that that mattered now. Bob's story agreed with his parents' in every way, and that seemed to preclude his murdering his sister at her house between seven-thirty and nine.

D.I. Pratt particularly wanted a look around the kitchen, professing a previously-unacknowledged interest in Chinese cuisine, although his naive questions must have indicated his apathy in that direction.

Bob had clearly not had time for the more mundane things in life the previous evening, as the dishes and ingredients were still scattered around the kitchen worktop and the sink. Despite his having been asked to go easy on the spices, there was a characteristically pungent smell that Pratt had often noticed outside Chinese takeaways.

Bob lived alone, and seemed to reserve most of his money for expensive electrical equipment and other gadgets (he had a large, fairly new BMW in his drive). All the ornaments in the lounge / dining-room appeared to be the sort that parents would give to their children, as they obviously did not fit in with Bob's style. His mother had mentioned that she particularly looked out for them when she called, but she felt he was the sort to keep them hidden and only bring them out when they visited. However, Pratt thought that that was what any son would do ... in fact, what he himself did.

Casually, not really sure for what reason, but thinking of the magazine, Pratt enquired, "Interested in practical electronics?"

"No," replied Bob lazily, "I prefer all my equipment ready-made."

So, where are we? thought Pratt. It was now late afternoon, and he was sitting in his car opposite what had been June New's house.

The doctors had confirmed the time of death. It had also been confirmed that June had been killed in the garage, and not moved from somewhere else.

There seemed little evidence to support a burglary, and no potential murderers had been unearthed by his staff ... apart from Bob, that is.

His parents surely wouldn't lie for him, certainly not when the victim had been their own beloved daughter?

One thing that worried Pratt was that June seemed to have acquired an interest in electronics without anyone else being aware. Or perhaps ...?

Pratt left his car, and walked across the road to the house. The copy of 'Practical Electronics' was still on the hall table. He looked at the cover, and found written near the top right-hand corner, "Dudley 46."

Bob lives at number 46, thought Pratt, although in another road some distance away. Could he be using the pseudonym of Dudley, and have left the magazine at June's house? No, that didn't explain anything.

Pratt decided to pop over to number 46 Aspen Avenue, and see if anyone called Dudley lived there, and whether he or she were interested in electronics.

Mr. Dudley was in a bad mood. Seeing the magazine in D.I. Pratt's hand, he clearly mistook him for the paper-boy's employer.

"And what happened to my evening paper yesterday?"

Pratt introduced himself, and explained what had happened.

"Delivered there, was it? We seem to get a new paper-boy every few weeks, and they don't know their way around."

"But what's up at number 38? We knew something was going on, because Mrs. New always puts her car in the garage as soon as she gets home, and she left it outside number 42 yesterday evening."

Pratt sat musing in his car.

So, one mystery was solved. The magazine had been intended for Mr. Dudley at number 46. But was there another mystery now? Why had June left her car outside number 42? Or wasn't it important?

In the rear-view mirror, he saw the paper-boy approaching. He got out of his car, and showed him his identification. The boy clearly seemed uneasy and was probably worried about some petty crime he'd once been involved in.

"Did you deliver the papers in this street yesterday, lad?" Pratt asked.

The boy nodded, "I usually do the other side of the estate, though. Was something wrong?" He didn't sound as if he really cared.

"I was wondering about 'Practical Electronics,' actually. Where did you deliver it?"

"I don't know. I do most of this on autopilot. I just look at the address Mr. Gibbons writes, and push the stuff through the letter-box."

"This was for number 46."

"That doesn't mean a lot to me, either. I've got enough to worry about with these fancy new ways of ordering house numbers. The papers yesterday were packed in house number order for this street, but I still had to shuffle around in my bag for some of them."

It was a little difficult getting anything other than hazy recollections out of the boy, so D.I. Pratt gave up, and let the relieved paper-boy continue on his round.

But at least things seemed to be a little clearer in Pratt's mind.

He drove back to Bob New's house. He thought his request might get a flat refusal, so, to save time, and as the BMW wasn't locked, he gently opened the boot. There was quite a large spillage of sweet-and-sour sauce on the carpeting in there.

Pratt's normal reaction would have been very restrained, but, this time, he yelled "Yes!" out loud. Suddenly realising where he was, he ducked, and moved back behind a tree before he was spotted.

But he needn't have worried unduly about Bob seeing him and then trying to remove any evidence. It would take a lot of work to get rid of that sauce.

Even when you know almost exactly what happened, it's often difficult to get all the evidence together to make a case, especially when you think it might stretch the credulity of a jury. Pratt had to work really hard.

Bob New had been intent on killing his sister for some time.

He had arranged an evening at his house for his parents. He would practise his new culinary abilities and cook a Chinese meal for them, and would provide transport to and from the station. They would be his alibi.

He had cooked the meal at his own house, 46 Presley Parade, late that afternoon, and had then put it, together with the cutlery and plates, in the boot of his BMW and driven to his sister's house (he had been careful not to take anything with a strong smell, although he had prepared plenty of aromatic side dishes to leave at his own house in order to give it the right ambience).

He had visited June's house, and had tied her up and gagged her in her garage. Then he had departed as prearranged to collect his parents, returning them to his sister's house. The house had exactly the same layout as Bob's … as had hundreds of other houses on the estate. But, before leaving for the station, Bob had been careful to cover up the house number with a plate marked '46,' which was why Mr. Dudley at 46 Aspen Avenue had had his 'Practical Electronics' delivered to the wrong house.

Anyway, Mr. and Mrs. New wouldn't have noticed the difference as long as the right ornaments were on display, and Bob had transferred those in the car boot, along with the meal.

The BMW would have been hidden in the garage to avoid attention, and so June's little Ford had had to be parked farther up the road.

It would only have taken a minute or so to murder June in the garage whilst "returning to the kitchen" (although, in reality, everything had been taken from and returned to the car boot).

So, all the mess and smell was in Bob's house (and car boot), and June's kitchen was almost spotless and odourless.

It was only when all this had been explained to Mr. and Mrs. New that they began to remember little things that had seemed different about their son's house ...

Chapter 17

The Toyshop that Moved

It was late on a cold Saturday night in November, and the rear lights of the last bus home were slowly and tantalisingly vanishing into the far distance.

John Marks cursed. He had been at a party at a large house on the Iffley Road. Normally, he was very good at time-keeping, but the party had been a good one. Whilst he had been careful not to over-imbibe to such a degree that he was unable to focus on his watch sufficiently to read the time, he had however drunk just enough for him not to realise that the damned thing had stopped several hours earlier.

The last bus having departed would not represent a problem for the students at the party, as they all had digs within a few yards of where it was being held, but John now had to find some way of getting to his newly-acquired flat in the hamlet of Prycham, several miles away. As his appointment as Junior Laboratory Technician at one of Oxford's newer colleges had been made only very recently at a probationary salary, he didn't think his bank manager would be very happy if he were to hire a taxi.

Thus he found himself reverting to his old student habits, and became resigned to having to thumb a lift, although it must be said that he hardly suffered waves of nostalgia over this.

Soon, however, after only a few minutes, he was rewarded by a large white van stopping for him. Clearly, he offered a more respectable aspect than when he had been a student.

"You going anywhere near Prycham?" he asked the young driver, who seemed almost the worse for drink as he was.

"Yeah, I've got to pass through it to get to Winterham," nodded the driver. "Hop in."

If the driver had been hoping to have company for the journey to Prycham, he must have been disappointed, for John fell into a doze almost the moment he sat down in the cab's warm interior. The combination of the warmth and the gentle rocking and the monotonous drone of the engine lulled him into the same feeling of drowsiness as he had felt when he had sat with his father many years ago in the front of the car.

He was awoken as the van came to a less than gentle stop, clearly intended by the driver to wake him up, and perhaps to punish him slightly for his unsuitability as a travelling companion.

"Prycham it is," intoned the driver, trying to lean over and open the passenger door, but not quite making it.

"Uh?" mumbled John as he tumbled out onto the pavement. "Er, thanks," he added, as he was engulfed in exhaust fumes. He sat down on a bench for a moment to clear his head.

Prycham looked like the archetypal picturesque late-mediaeval Oxfordshire village, but had in fact been built in the late nineteenth century by a factory owner, whose large and unpicturesque factory was a mile upstream. Built of local stone, each house had been designed to resemble a suitably ancient and picturesque building from the region, and the whole village had been laid out symmetrically around the River Pyshe. The village had originally been built to house the workers from the factory, but no factory-worker could afford the houses now, and they were all occupied by estate agents and financial consultants who worked in Oxford.

The driver had set John down at one end of the only bridge in the centre of Prycham. As he gradually began to become aware of the cold, John noticed a toyshop he had never seen before. It was on the opposite side of the river, in a row of terraced houses and shops. The very top part of the window had a large clown's face painted on it, smiling irresistibly down on any child who might wish to be enticed.

He ambled across the bridge towards the toyshop.

It was everything he could imagine a child in bygone times could wish for in a toyshop. There were no electrical items, and most of the toys seemed to be solidly built of wood.

There were wooden pull-along trains and cars on shelves to the left, whilst dolls and woollen toys graced those on the opposite wall. Items for baby were carefully strewn around the floor in front of the window, and he could see prams (under a sign "Perambulators") lining the back wall, where an archway promised further delights towards the back of the shop. Behind the baby toys at the front, a number of fancy-dress costumes were draped over some chairs.

Then John noticed that one of the fancy-dress costumes was a little different to the others. In fact it seemed to be a large, life-size puppet. A rather ugly puppet, which John thought unusual.

If one were making a puppet, wouldn't one use a pleasant, friendly, funny, or at worst an agreeably villainous face?

Surely one wouldn't use a face as ugly as this one? There was even a long scar from the right eye half-way down the cheek, which vaguely resembled a duelling scar. He thought briefly of one of Dickens' Christmas stories, in which there was a toymaker who hated children and always painted ugly faces on his dolls. But that was a story. Surely nobody who wanted to make money would do that?

Then he noticed a large patch of what looked like blood on the white shirt of the puppet.

Almost instinctively, he moved towards the door, and went to open it. Surprisingly, it opened at his touch.

The puppet was just inside the door.

But it was human.

And it was also most definitely dead.

He stopped and thought. A murderer might be on the premises. So perhaps it would be best not to go farther into the shop. He decided to do what people never do in films, and decided to phone the police.

He walked away from the shop, deciding it would not be wise to hunt around for a phone inside.

He noted the position of the shop as carefully as his inebriated state allowed. It was a small single shop that stood at the rightmost end of a row of small, terraced houses, with another small shop that matched the toyshop at the other end of the terrace.

He hadn't lived in Prycham for long, and didn't know the layout of the village that well. The only part he knew was the route from his place of work to his flat. Leaving Oxford, he would take the route the van driver had taken to Prycham, would turn left across the bridge over the river, and then would turn left again, onto a long cul-de-sac that lead to Parchington. His flat was about half-a-mile along this road.

As this was the centre of the village, he reasoned that there must be a telephone kiosk fairly near.

Eventually he did find one, and was surprised to find it was working.

"Hello, Police?"

The policeman on the other end of the line admitted it was.

"My name is John Marks. Look, this may sound strange, but I've just looked into a shop window, a toyshop window, by the bridge in Prycham, and there's a dead body in the shop." He realised he was gabbling a little.

The policeman seemed to accept this more readily than he would have expected.

"I'll send a car out. Where might we find you?"

"I'll wait on the bridge in the centre of the village. That way I can watch the shop," John said.

He retraced his steps past the toyshop, and leant on the parapet of the bridge.

It was bitterly cold. Nevertheless, he was having difficulty in staying awake and was feeling decidedly sick. He sat down on the pavement.

He was woken up by a police officer shaking his shoulder.

"Are you John Marks?"

John nodded blearily.

"You reported seeing a dead body in a toyshop?"

John nodded again, less blearily.

He got up, and they started to walk to where the police officer had parked his car by the end of the bridge.

John pointed to the shop on the right at the end of the terrace. "That's it."

He looked through the shop window. There were shelves and shelves lined with tins of food. There was a chilled food counter that stretched from near the front of the shop towards the back. There was a large soft drinks cabinet on the right, and, beyond that, a section for alcoholic drinks. In short, it was the sort of general grocery shop that was faster-than-gradually dying out, as the ubiquitous supermarkets began to take over almost everywhere.

But there were no toys, no perambulators, no dolls …

… and certainly no blood-stained puppets.

"With varying vanities, from every part, they shift the moving toyshop of their heart," muttered the police officer.

"You read Pope?" asked John surprised.

"No, Crispin," replied the police officer.

John wasn't asked to come to the station to make a statement. However, he did have to endure a long lecture about wasting police time and "going easy on the drink, Sir."

Rather guiltily, he accepted the offer of a lift back to his flat, although he insisted that he be dropped some distance away, in order to retain some degree of anonymity after his embarrassing brush with the law.

By the following evening, although he felt much better and more clear-headed, he still had no idea what had happened the night before. Had he imagined or dreamt it all, or at least the bit about the toyshop? He had only just moved back into a student environment, and he found that living with his parents again for the previous two years had severely impaired his ability to handle his drink. But surely he hadn't drunk that much?

If he had seen what he thought he had, it was perhaps possible that someone had changed the appearance of the shop after his original visit, although they would only have had a very short time in which to do it. In fact, it would have had to have been done whilst he was making the phone call and waiting for the police officer. That wasn't possible, surely?

And why would anybody change the identity of a shop? John couldn't think why, but he was still sure he had not been mistaken.

In fact, he was so convinced that he actually called into the local police station that evening to reaffirm his beliefs.

The desk sergeant there listened patiently, but was also disinclined to take a statement. There had been no reports of anyone missing or dead, and so there seemed little point. He saw no reason to try and trace the van driver. Not reassured, John returned to his flat. Perhaps another night's sleep might help.

Of course it didn't.

He awoke even more confused each morning that week.

"Brigadoon," muttered Aunt Gwendolyn.

"What?" said John, rather disinterestedly. He had heard far too many of Aunt Gwendolyn's ramblings to take much of anything she said seriously.

"Brigadoon. It's that Scottish village that comes to life every hundred years. It's a musical by Rodgers and Hammersmith.'"

"Once every century, this little Scottish village comes to life, and outsiders can venture in and meet and talk to the local people. That's just like your toyshop. Perhaps the grocery shop only turns into the toyshop every hundred years, or every ten years, or perhaps every week."

John muttered something noncommittally, and then changed the subject.

But there might be something, albeit very little, in what Aunt Gwendolyn had said, John thought. He usually visited her on his way home from shopping late each Saturday afternoon, and this was the first Saturday after his sighting of the phantom toyshop.

Maybe if he just waited near the bridge, not too close to the shop itself, he might see something.

His Aunt lived just down the road from his flat, near to the end of the road at Parchington. After visiting her, he dropped his shopping off at the flat, and then walked to the bridge over the little river in the centre of the village.

He stayed on his side of the river, and took up position across the road from the bridge, near a signpost that pointed (for those crossing the bridge from the Oxford side) right to Winterham and left to "Parchington (no through road)." He found a position where he was sheltered slightly, so that he could clearly see the grocery shop on the road to Oxford, but could not, or so he hoped, easily be seen from the other side.

He waited. It had been dark now for some time, and, this being mid-evening on a cold November night, there was little traffic. Most people seemed to be saving both their money and their excesses for the following month.

He began to feel foolish. What if a friend or colleague saw him hiding in the shadows by the bridge? Would he, or, rather, *could* he explain his reasons? He certainly wouldn't be stupid enough to mention his Aunt Gwendolyn and Brigadoon.

Two cars, clearly in convoy, crossed the bridge from Oxford and turned towards Winterham. They might have been lost, as the lead driver stopped briefly to look at the signpost near the bridge. John pushed himself even further into the shadows in case one of the drivers tried to ask directions. But the occupants all started laughing loudly, and the two cars roared off into the night.

A large white van, not the one in which John had kindly been given a lift the week before, came along the road from Oxford, and drove straight on without crossing the bridge. John wasn't sure to where that road led, and resolved to look at the road sign on the other side of the bridge some time.

The two cars in convoy returned, shot over the bridge, and headed off in the same direction as the white van.

After a few minutes, another van appeared from the direction of Oxford, crossed the bridge, and then indicated right for Winterham.

And then, almost miraculously, the toyshop appeared.

It was unmistakable.

Although looking for the most part like any other shop in the area, there was the clown's face over the front window. It still smiled down enticingly.

And then, in a flash, it was gone.

John blinked, but the toyshop was no longer there.

He looked around, bemused. To his left, the van was picking up speed towards Winterham. Across its rear was emblazoned 'Winterham and District Glaziers.'

Glaziers?

Glass?

John looked again.

He could see that there were large panes of glass secured to the nearside of the van. As the van drove off towards Winterham, there was a flash as one of the few street lights in the village was reflected in the glass.

Reflected?

Could the toyshop really be only a reflection?

John looked across the river to the grocery shop. Then he turned left towards Winterham.

It was only now, as he began to explore a little more of the village in which he had recently started living, that John began to realise just how symmetrical the village was. Prycham had been developed as one man's ideal community, and the half of the village on one side of the river almost exactly mirrored that on the other. The terraced houses and shops on this side of the bridge seemed almost identical to those on the other side. Where the grocery shop was on the road to Oxford, on this side, also at the rightmost end of the terrace, was a toyshop. No, thought John, *the* toyshop.

In his rather drunken state the previous Saturday, John realised he must have got confused about which end of the bridge he had been dropped off at. He must have got out of the van on the Oxford side of the bridge, not the Parchington side, and so the toyshop was actually on the Winterham Road, not the Oxford Road as he thought.

He might have been further disorientated when he was woken up in the middle of the bridge by the police officer.

But the toyshop seemed innocuous enough. He could now see that the name 'Couch and Co.' was written above the clown's face painted on the front window. Inside could be glimpsed the wooden pull-along trains and cars, the dolls and woollen toys, the baby goods and prams, the fancy-dress costumes, and the other things he remembered … but this time there was no ugly, blood-stained puppet to be seen.

Had he really been expecting to see one? he thought.

On Sunday morning, he felt it was time to visit the local police station again.

It might have been wiser to have forgotten all about it, now that he knew why his toyshop had 'moved.'

But his reception at the police station was not what he had expected.

"Thank God you've called in," exclaimed the sergeant on duty. "Young Phillips and the desk sergeant you saw have really been hauled over the coals about neglecting to take your name and address."

John felt reassured.

"The thing is," continued the desk sergeant, "A day or two after you'd called in, we had a phone call from the Couch brothers to say their father had gone away for the week at a small cottage the family owns in Yorkshire. They said they knew he'd arrived there because he phoned them up early on Saturday evening, but they hadn't heard from him since, and, as some friends who lived locally had called in and only found his luggage there, they were beginning to get worried."

"His body was found in some woods near the cottage yesterday."

"It looked pretty suspicious, and the Couch Brothers have a bad reputation and plenty of motive. But we needed some further evidence to back our ideas up."

"And I think you may be able to give it to us."

"Did Mr. Couch have a long scar from the right eye half-way down his cheek?" John asked.

The desk sergeant smiled and nodded.

Chapter 18

There's a Way

D.I. John Pratt, off duty for once, and Roger Payne sat together in a corner of the 'Aleford Tea Rooms.' Until a year previously, they would usually have been found in the bar of the 'Crown and Parsnip,' but Roger had been advised by his doctor to give up alcohol, and he found the lure of being in the pub too strong. Of his many drinking companions, only John had decided to keep him company, although it must be said that this was hardly on a regular basis.

"Look, I'm not trying to be avaricious, but there's no way that my father would have wanted any of his money to go to Simon," Roger mumbled into his teacup.

He certainly did look more upset that his father's wishes might be ignored than that he might be swindled out of some money, thought John.

"Simon has always had money of his own, well, ever since an uncle left all his inheritance to him … and I don't know why I wasn't included in that, to be honest. But recently he had this almighty bust-up with Dad, and Dad told me he was cutting him out of his will. So he made a new will, more or less on his death-bed, and tried to leave it all to me. But Simon contested the new will successfully, and now he's still getting half … and that's not what Dad wanted."

"So, on what grounds did he contest the will?" asked John.

"Well, as I said, my father was in a blind fury with Simon, and wanted things done as quickly as possible. So he made up the will himself. He had completed his previous wills that way - I don't think he trusted solicitors much - and they must have been done correctly, because his previous will still stands. But this one he told me he had got two of his employees from the farm to witness it. It all seemed all right."

"Anyway, he died the night afterwards. There were no suspicious circumstances, and, to be frank, it was more or less expected."

"But the will was contested by Simon, and we found that the signatures on the will weren't valid. They hired a handwriting expert who said that there was no way that the two staff named on the will as witnesses could have produced those signatures. And yet my father told me categorically that they had actually signed the will."

"Hang on, "John interrupted, "Let's get this in some sort of order." He'd already heard bits of the story from various other sources.

"Your father had the big argument on ...?"

"Monday," answered Roger.

"And he told you on Tuesday evening that he'd just changed his will?" John looked at Roger, who nodded, "And that he had asked two farm employees to act as witnesses?"

Roger nodded again, "John Davis and Andrew Gregg."

"And what do *they* say?" enquired John.

"Well, they admit that my father asked them in and explained what he wanted, but they claim he said he'd ask them to sign later. They say they never actually signed the will."

"But Dad was so definite about it," continued Roger. "He said they had signed. He must have seen them do it."

"Are these farmhands trustworthy?"

"I would have thought so. They've always been very honest and loyal to my father. They're local lads, so probably Simon would know them better than I. I spent my childhood in boarding-schools, but Simon grew up in the village."

"So, could there be another will, the one that they signed?"

"There's no chance of that, I'm afraid. Dad entrusted the will into my safe-keeping immediately afterwards. I made sure it couldn't be tampered with."

"So, now, everyone either thinks that my father forgot to ask them to sign, and then signed in their absence, or, worse still, that I tried to change the will with forged signatures."

John sat quietly with his eyes closed, and didn't say anything for a while. Roger assumed that he was hinting that it was his round, so he got up and went to the counter to order another two cups of tea (the normal practice here was waitress service, but Roger and John were used to going to the bar for drinks).

"You're not very popular with the farm staff, are you?" John said, as he finally opened his eyes. He looked surprised that another cup of tea had materialised in front of him, especially so since Roger had also provided a 'chaser,' in the form of a small cupcake.

"Well, it's not that. It's just that I've not been involved with the farm much. Not that Simon really has either, but he's certainly been more of a resident here than I have."

"Well, assuming your father was compos mentis, as it were, there's only one real solution, isn't there?"

"Which is ...?" prompted Roger.

"Well, Simon must have got the farmhands onto his side, probably with some story about his half-share being his birthright, and your trying to cut him out of the will by telling lies to your father. Perhaps there was some suggestion of there being a percentage in it for them also."

"But the handwriting expert assured me that the signatures weren't in their handwriting," countered Roger, any feeling of renewed hope having rapidly dissipated. "He said he would have known even if they had tried to disguise their writing. And we even got a second opinion to be absolutely sure."

"And your father was certain that they had signed the will."

"He was definite," confirmed Roger.

"So they must have signed each other's names."

"Eh?"

"Well, your father would be satisfied that they'd signed as witnesses, but any handwriting expert would confirm that John Davis hadn't signed his own name, and neither had Andrew Gregg ... but if they'd signed each other's names ..."

"Yes," beamed Roger Payne, "And our handwriting experts should be able to prove that."

John Pratt sat back. "I think merely the threat of exposure should be enough to make the farm-hands admit their deception."

Roger went off to get another round of drinks.

Chapter 19

Mrs. Gossip

"Aha! Here comes Hercules."

Harry "Sarge" Pottle was the desk sergeant at the small police station in Pentlesham, and his referring to D.I. John Pratt as Hercules wasn't a reference to his strength, rather than to John's love of detective stories, in particular those written by Agatha Christie. It also suggested Sarge's almost total ignorance of them.

"Anything happening?" asked John, although he wasn't expecting much, as there was never a great deal in the way of real crime in such a rural community. He was actually only making a courtesy call before visiting an elderly relative who lived nearby.

"I've just the thing," said Sarge. He hunted under the desk and eventually brought out a letter. "I doubt you can do much with this though." He winked to nobody in particular.

"It's a poison-pen letter," said John, a little disappointed.

"Aye," agreed Sarge, "And, as the letter was printed from a computer and not handwritten, you won't be able to deduce much from that."

"And that's where you're wrong," explained John. "In a rural area like this, how many of the sort of people who would write a letter like this would have a computer? I mean, you could hardly ask a relative or a friend to type it up and print it out for you, could you?"

"And that's where *you're* wrong," replied Sarge, happily. "There's a course every Monday evening right here in the village hall, run by a rather handsome - or so I gather - young man from the local university. 'Computers for Stupid People' it's called, or something like that. It's very popular, especially with the older folk, and especially with the ladies. So, if you asked me to compile a list of all the people whom I suspect might want to write such a letter, I could write down about twenty names. And nineteen of those on the list would be able to type and print off such a letter."

John felt a little crestfallen, so he ignored Sarge's gaze, and read the letter carefully.

"To whom it may concern –

Doesn't anybody in our village worry about Harry Sadler, our lovable local Bank Manager? Doesn't anybody care about the safety of our dear innocent children? Why is Mr. Sadler allowed every lunchtime to wander from his place of work to the park alongside the local school? Why is he allowed to sit on the bench overlooking the sports area and ogle the young girls in their sports clothes whilst happily munching his gossip sandwiches? Shouldn't something be done? Shouldn't we villagers get together and force the Police to do something? BEFORE IT'S TOO LATE!

Mrs. Gossip"

John put the paper down on the desk.

"No fingerprints" said Sarge, again happily.

"How much of this is true?" asked John.

"Well, everything in the letter is true, because it doesn't really say anything, does it? Harry Sadler is our Bank Manager. He does eat his sandwiches on the bench by the girls playing netball, or whatever. But it's the only bench there since the one on the other side of the park was vandalised and burnt a few months ago." He shrugged his shoulders.

John picked up the letter and re-read it.

"There's one strange thing about this," he said. "The whole letter is very matter-of-fact throughout … except for one point, where it becomes almost surreal."

"The idea of Mr. Sadler eating gossip sandwiches," suggested Sarge.

"Yes," agreed John, "It's rather odd, and more than a little bizarre."

John thought for a moment.

"Could you write down that list of possible suspects for me, please?" he said. "And I'll try and predict who our poison-pen letter-writer is."

It was Sarge's turn to be thoughtful. He wrote down a few names, then looked into space for a while and wrote down a few more.

"Is nineteen enough?" he asked, a smirk on his face.

"So who's our Mrs. Gossip?" he prompted.

John felt like a conjuror who was about to reveal the name of the card a member of the audience had chosen.

"Well," he said, "I very much doubt that there's a Mrs. Cheese there."

Sarge smiled and shook his head, as if he expected failure all along and was relishing it.

"So, let's go with Mrs. Ham then," said John with a flourish that suggested rather more confidence than he actually felt.

"Jean Ham?" spluttered Sarge. "She's certainly on the list. And one of the more likely candidates, if not THE most likely candidate."

"OK, I'm sure we can stop all this if we visit her. But you've got to give me some proof, John, or at least some idea why you chose her name out of the proverbial hat."

John wondered how best to explain it. "Well, it really revolved around those gossip sandwiches. That phrase was rather too surreal to fit in with such an otherwise plainly-written letter."

"Then it occurred to me that the writer might have originally decided to use her real name, but then chickened out at the last minute. Instead of just changing her name from Mrs. Ham to Mrs. Gossip, she used a global "replace all" change …"

"… And poor Mr. Sadler's ham sandwiches became surreal," continued Sarge, thoughtfully for once.

"OK, I think I'll call in on our Mrs. Ham this afternoon."

"And one final point," said John as he went off to visit his relative, "I think I'd also find out whether our Mr. Sadler has an alibi for when the other park bench was vandalised and burnt."

Sarge was left thinking for while, before picking up the station phone.

Chapter 20

Off the Rails

The railway line from Aleford to the small village of Meadow Cloud runs in an almost perfectly straight line for twelve miles, leading some folk to think it might be an old Roman railway line. There are no stops until the line reaches Meadow Cloud, when a sharp, almost ninety-degree turn means trains have to slow right down on the approach to the station. The reason for this was that nineteenth-century plans for the station to be built to the west of the village had been blocked by the influential local gentry at the last minute, and the station had had to be relocated.

So, northbound train-drivers have to start slowing down immediately after Daemon's Bridge. And, fortunately, that's exactly what Ted Simmons, the driver of the 1615 train from Aleford to Wilchester, was doing.

It was less fortunate that platelayers on the line had not secured one of the lengths of rail properly after their last repair.

Ted Simmons noticed that something looked wrong, and braked sharply. He felt the train lurch slightly, before coming to rest a short distance farther on. It remained upright. It could have been worse, he thought, as there was a deep concrete culvert alongside the track at this point.

Ted hoped that the few passengers on board the two-carriage train would be unhurt. His main worry was for the small number of passengers who might have stood up in readiness to alight at the station.

Slightly shocked, he tried to stand, but fell over and hit his head against something hard. So, for a few minutes, he just sat in his compartment. He felt he needed to rest for a while.

The accident had been so quiet and gentle that not even those waiting at Meadow Cloud Station had realised that an incident had taken place.

The first person on the scene was from one of the two houses that stood opposite each other at one end of Daemon's Bridge. As they overlooked the cutting through which the train had just passed, the noise was reflected up in their direction.

Harry Andrews was first to reach the carriages.

He ran up to the second carriage, which was still on the rails. Everyone on board was seated. Perhaps no-one in there had wanted to get off at Meadow Cloud.

The first carriage was a different matter. Harry's attention was drawn to an open door, where an elderly gentleman was standing, leaning against the door-frame for support. He had blood trickling from his forehead, and he looked as if he might be concussed. Harry spoke to him for a minute or two and settled him into a seat, and then looked around the carriage. Almost everyone else was seated, some nursing their heads. Four passengers were lying on the floor, clearly having fallen over after getting up to leave the train at Meadow Cloud Station. None seemed badly hurt.

"Dilys!" yelled Harry as he looked around the carriage. He bobbed down to look below the seats, but still seemed unable to see for whom he was looking.

"Dilys!" he yelled again, before turning away from the carriage and looking around the surrounding area.

"Oh God!" he screamed, and climbed down into the culvert. A bloodied and shabbily-dressed body was lying at the bottom.

Overweight and out-of-condition, D.C.I. Jolliffe was to retire soon, and had been hoping for an easy last few months. Initially, he had hoped that this would be a simple case, straightforward enough to be quickly handed over to someone else to tie up the loose ends.

After all, the accident had not been that serious, and there had initially appeared to be only cuts and bruises …

… But then Dilys Andrews had been found at the bottom of the culvert.

It looked as if she had been standing at the door, waiting to disembark, when the jerk of the train derailing had made her turn her hand, and she had fallen out of the door into the culvert.

Now statements had to be taken.

D.C.I. Jolliffe insisted on having D.I. John Pratt to assist him. He was much younger and better suited to all the legwork that this case might demand. He was also intelligent enough to be able to make a lot of the decisions himself.

Ted Simmons was very upset, as he seemed to think the whole matter reflected badly upon his unblemished record with the railway company. No doubt there would be recriminations against the track maintenance teams, but that wasn't the main focus at the moment.

Ted sobbed a little, "I had slowed down, far slower than they insisted on. I know just how tight that curve is, and I always take no chances there. It's a nasty curve that."

"Still, I thought nobody would have been hurt. I didn't have chance to leave my seat to check for a while …"

D.C.I. Jolliffe interrupted, "That's a very nasty cut you have on your head, Mr. Simmons. Nobody blames you for anything."

Ted continued as if he hadn't been listening, "If only there hadn't been people getting off at Meadow Cloud. If they'd all been seated … but, of course, everybody wants to get off quickly, so they all crowd around the doors, some with their hands on the handles, all ready to get off …"

Matthew Ainslie was the elderly gentlemen whom Harry had found standing near an open door. He had been slightly concussed.

"I'm afraid I was eager to get off the train as usual, standing by the door all ready to turn the handle. That last slow run into the station can be so frustrating."

"But I'm afraid I don't remember much about it."

"Well, you were concussed," said Jolliffe.

"Yes. But I could still think fairly clearly though. Enough to be able to find and hand over my ticket anyway."

"Is there anything else you can add?" asked D.I. Pratt.

"Not really. Almost everyone remained calm. There were a few on the floor. They'd been waiting to get off too, but all those seated were fine, apart from a few hysterical old maids. And then there was poor Mrs. Andrews …"

Quick statements had been taken from everyone on the train, to be followed up later if that were deemed necessary.

All these other statements agreed with Mr. Ainslie's account.

Harry Andrews they had questioned last, to give him time to come to terms with his loss.

"Dilys had decided to set off early and spend the day shopping in Aleford. Shopping or just looking around. Something like that, anyway. She rarely does that, so it's a bit of a treat for her, I suppose."

"I was doing the gardening in the patch that overlooks the railway line, so I knew what had happened straight away. I just knew that Dilys would be on board that train."

"I raced across the bridge and down the other side, and then ran between the line and that culvert …"

His voice trailed off a little.

"Anyway, the accident was so slight that I assumed she'd be on board safe and sound. I looked in the second carriage, the one that was still on the track, but she wasn't in there."

"Then I went to help an elderly gentleman in the first carriage. He seemed OK, if a little dazed. There was still no sign of Dilys, so I began to hope she had caught a later train. I looked around, and then I saw …"

He smiled weakly.

"I think the ambulance men must have thought me the most hysterical of the lot."

He laughed and then went silent.

Jolliffe looked at his notes, and then said "Well, I think that's all we'll be needing for the moment. We'll call up to you if we need anything else."

"Oh, one question … where were the people that live in the house opposite you at the time?"

Harry Andrews shrugged. "I have no idea. The sound of the accident was very slight. I only heard it because I was at the bottom of the garden. Perhaps the Listers didn't hear anything."

Jolliffe opened his notebook, and then closed it decisively.

"Well, I don't think there's anything here we need worry about. An open-and-shut case, eh?"

D.I. Pratt thought deeply. He shook his head.

"I just have a bad feeling about all this. Would somebody, her husband perhaps, want to murder Dilys Andrews?"

"I don't know," replied Jolliffe, "I wasn't married to her."

"Look," he added, "Are you suggesting that her husband deliberately derailed the train in order to kill his wife?"

"That only happens in films, I'm sure," replied Pratt. "Either way, how could he have been certain that his wife would be killed? She was the only one more than even slightly injured."

Pratt shook his head again. "No, the first thing that worries me is that Harry said she spent all day in Aleford, and yet, despite appeals, nobody has come forward to say they saw her there."

"But she did have a valid ticket on her," muttered Jolliffe. "Anyway, Aleford's a big town. People in big towns don't notice other people these days. Aleford's not like a small village in the country, such as Meadow Cloud. There again, sometimes you can wander around here all day without anybody seeing you."

"And I have one final niggling worry," continued Pratt.

"If she had gone shopping, why was she wearing what looked like gardening clothes?"

"I don't know," muttered Jolliffe, "But different people have different standards. Maybe that was smart for her."

"Either way, you've got a suspicious mind, Pratt," said Jolliffe, "You'll go far."

Jolliffe was still keen to close the case, but he agreed to Pratt's request to visit Daemon's Bridge to have another chat with Harry and also with the Listers.

Harry was gardening again, and was happy to show the two policemen his patch. It did indeed overlook the railway line. If this had been a film, thought Pratt, a train would have passed by whilst they were standing there, but there were very few trains each day now.

Mrs. Lister was very friendly. Her husband had been away, and she had stayed in her house all day with Vivaldi. Pratt looked around, but could see no hi-fi.

Suddenly an immerse and unruly white Labrador ran in. "Down, Vivaldi!"" screamed Mrs. Lister.

After almost an hour, Jolliffe and Pratt were finally able to make their escape. They had only heard platitudes and gossip, unfortunately none of which related to the case in hand. Pratt had at least learnt something interesting about his old history teacher, Mr. Douglas.

"So, are you happy to let the case drop now, Pratt?" asked Jolliffe.

"I'd just like to check one last thing, if you don't mind," replied Pratt.

He continued, "Did you notice that the window-boxes at Harry's house had recently been well watered, quite sloppily too …"

"What has that got to do with anything?" asked Jolliffe.

"… And that there was water all over the window-sills at the Listers' house too, as if someone had tried to water window-boxes there too …"

"What the hell are you on about, Pratt?" screamed Jolliffe. He was now red in the face.

"… And yet the Listers don't have any window-boxes at all," smiled Pratt.

"Ah, now I get it," smiled Jolliffe.

"You do?" said Pratt, pleased.

"OF COURSE I BLOODY DON'T," yelled Jolliffe.

"Hang on," said Pratt, "I just want to ask Mrs. Lister a question."

He ran back to the house and then returned, scribbling something on a piece of paper.

"I think I know how to find this guy," he said. "The local newsagent should have his address."

Will Beer was at home. He was the local window-cleaner, who had cycled out to Daemon's Bridge on the day of the rail accident to make a little money at the two houses there.

"Yes," he said when he had let the two policemen into his front, and only, room, "I got paid at both houses. Mr. Andrews was in the garden as usual, but Mrs. Andrews paid me. Three o'clock it was."

Pratt grinned.

Jolliffe just looked bemused.

Outside the house, Pratt explained.

"It's simple, really. Harry heard the crash, and went with his wife to see if they could help. Nobody would have seen them between the house and the train. When they got there, he took advantage of the situation."

"He threw her into the culvert."

"Then he checked the carriages, leaving one extra door open, and went to help the elderly gentleman. He must have asked for his ticket, which, in his concussed state, he would have been happy to give him."

"Then Harry climbed down into the culvert, and put the ticket in his wife's pocket."

"I just hope he didn't find the need to finish her off."

By the same Author

The Return of Inspector Pirat: His First Book

Paperback available on Amazon
www.amazon.co.uk/Return-Inspector-Pirat-First-Book/dp/1511429461/

eBook available on Amazon
www.amazon.co.uk/Return-Inspector-Pirat-First-Book-ebook/dp/B00UTKEKPM/

"The Return of Inspector Pirat : His First Book" (published in 2015) is a series of apparently-unrelated detective short stories, but with a link that may not become apparent until the final chapter.

A college professor with a passion for detective fiction annually invites those of his students who are similarly-inclined along to his house for an evening of good food, well-chosen wine, and, hopefully, inspired story-telling.

Each of twenty students reads out his or her story to the others, the stories being interspersed with moments of inebriation, passion and fleas …

Visit Rob's website:
www.robertfalconer.co.uk/